For the Sake of Freedom

By L.T. World

Printed in the United States of America

FIRST EDITION

ISBN: 978-1-952352-14-0

Published by:

Crave Press

www.cravepress.com

Dedication

To the friends and family who helped me know God and his teachings.

Surely, you would not, in this age of scientific enlightenment, declare that God or nature has marked some pleasures as "moral" or "good" and others as "immoral" or "bad"? In any case, let me assure you, my dear young lady, that there is absolutely no comparison between the pleasure that I might take in eating ham and the pleasure I anticipate in raping and murdering you. That is the honest conclusion to which my education has led me–after the most conscientious examination of my spontaneous and uninhibited.

~ Ted Bundy cited in Louis P. Pojman, *Ethics: Discovering Right and Wrong*, 3rd edition, Wadsworth/Thomson, 1999, pp. 31-32.

Introduction

Year 2250

Sitting next to his son at the edge of a lake, Christian holds a crystal in his hand. The crystal is tranquil blue with crimson wires like veins running through it. Smog chokes the distant area. Orbis City is several miles away. Christian only traveled as far as he needed to from the city, hoping for his son to return when possible. A low-flying aircraft, about the size of a go-kart, speeds over the closest hill. It nears the lake.

Looking over at his son, Christian smiles tenderly while holding his hand, “Are you ready, Oliver?”

Watching the aircraft approach, Oliver nods, “I am, Father.”

Weaving through the trees like a flying beetle, the aircraft finds a patch of grass to settle on. A frantic woman raises the glass cockpit and hops out. She runs towards Christian shouting, “It’s happening! It’s happening!”

“Calm down, Cynthia,” Christian says with a hand in the air. “You have come to tell me about Adam, correct?”

“Yes, I have,” Cynthia says, trying to catch her breath, “it’s all just so unreal. I’m sure you already know about it, because you know everything.”

Chuckling, Christian nods as he replies, “Yes, I do,” then sobering, continues, “it is awful business. Please, for your own sake, explain to me what is happening. That way you can process it for yourself.”

"After you left, Adam launched his new Protection Protocol initiative. Those parasites, as I like to call them, were released but weren't activated. They have been today."

"Why are you afraid?"

"Why am I afraid? Damn. I would like to know why you aren't." Cynthia bites her lip and pauses.

"You know why I'm not," Christian replies quietly.

"Yes, I know. I'm afraid because this could be the end. The end! I saw what those parasites, or rovers, as they call them, can do. They can collect personal information just by face recognition, sneak into people's homes, track people using everyone's microchips, and suck blood which is why I call them parasites. Why they need blood types, I'll never know."

"So, explain to me again why you're afraid."

Sighing, Cynthia sits down with her face buried in her hands. She replies, "There's already civil unrest. People are scared and starting to riot, but worst of all, I know that Orbis is hiding something."

"The plague," Oliver whispers.

"Yes," Cynthia responds, "you two do know everything, don't you?"

The crystal glows in Christian's hand as he smiles. Setting it by the water, he rises to his feet to stretch.

Oliver says, "Europe's prime minister had his own personal Rover. He said it served him better than any guard or servant ever could. His blood cells are mutating, and he is predicted to have only a few days left to live. Despite concerns about their product, Orbis denies all responsibility, claiming their tests have been thorough. That, we both know, is a lie."

Cynthia nods. She says, "I know they ignored results, but today they activated all of those deadly parasites, not just one special one for the prime minister."

"War and pestilence are coming within a week. The world as we know it will end, but Orbis will survive."

"It will?"

"Yes, but just like a man jumping out of a tower. He may survive, but only as a paralytic."

Kicking the crystal into the water, Christian along with the others watch it flash crimson. Then, like a supernova, the crystal explodes with a burst of light. Oliver and Christian stare into the pool of water, but Cynthia must cover her eyes. Afterwards, within seconds, like an invisible dome covering the lake and surrounding greenery, a new sort of life seeped through the landscape. The water became clear and the vegetation spread its leaves with new life. Uncovering her eyes, Cynthia looks around with awe.

"It's too bad I must leave," Cynthia whispers.

"You don't have to," Christian says, "you could stay and discover how life was meant to be lived. The vision I had for it."

Glancing over her shoulder at the smog where Orbis lies, Cynthia groans. She looks back at Christian and says, "But it costs me everything I know. You told me I'd have to leave behind so many things to know your vision. To have your new life. There are certain things worth dying for, you know?"

"Yes, of course," Olvier replies. "I know very well there are things worth dying for, but foolish pleasure is not one of them. Let go of those drugs, fornicators, and idols, the gods you worship. Instead, know true joy."

Looking over her shoulder again, Cynthia frowns. She stares at Oliver and says, "You don't understand how they make me feel. They are worth it."

"So be it. We will not stop you from returning."

"Must I leave now? I would like to stay just for a little bit."

"The time has come for you to decide, Cynthia. You cannot stay here with a divided heart. You must leave or stay wholly."

Nodding gravely, Cynthia hesitates then turns. She walks for her aircraft.

"By the way," Oliver calls out. Cynthia turns around curious. "They wanted blood to make a new man

— a new life. It only led to death. Remember, Orbis only leads to death."

Flipping off Oliver, Cynthia hops into the cockpit and flies away, never to return.

Chapter 1

Jotting down notes, Chase Hartford fixes his glasses. Seated between a microscope and a thick notepad, he presses his eye against the microscope's eyepiece. His bony fingers, protected by taut skin, fiddle with his pen. Hastily scribbling notes, like a true doctor, he mutters gibberish beneath his breath. Cold air trickles down Chase's spine, raising the hairs on the back of his neck. Bach's masterpiece "Inventions and Sinfonias" plays softly in the background, pervading the room.

"Ahh," Chase whispers, quickly writing down more notes. Slouched over his notepad like a possessive troll, he pages through some of his previous entries. Squinting, he mouths the words to himself. White lights only bright enough to cast a dim glow whir and flicker. Their neighbors, moaning vents, sputter cold air. Scratching his thinning black hair, Chase sits back in his chair. A shadow swallows the left side of his narrow face. The other side, angled towards the nearest light, resembles a ghastly pale ghoul. Harrowing, it would cause children to weep. His hollow eyes, hand-crafted by the devil, destroy light like black holes. His sunken cheeks cradle a pack of unsightly moles. At the end of his face, he boasts a sharp chin.

Staring at the microscope, Chase bites his dusty lip. Freezers, like filing cabinets, circle the room. Organized numerically, the set of stainless-steel freezers behind Chase ranges from one to ten. The columns proceed similarly until the last column of freezers ends with the number 1,000. The sample currently under the microscope has a 287 sticker on the glass cover. Cracking his crisp knuckles, Chase licks his lips.

"Dr. Hartford," an androgynous voice croaks over crackly intercoms, "Dr. Morey would like to speak with you."

Reaching underneath the table, Chase flips a switch. A microphone snakes out from underneath the table, stopping at Chase's mouth.

"Thank you, Skyler," Chase says, his voice is dry like sandpaper, "I will see him right away." Shutting the mic off, he rises from the table, setting the sample in a small freezer drawer by his knee. He places the sample between many others in a row titled "In-Progress." Scooping his notebook into the crook of his arm, he turns the lights off, dials the music to mute, and locks the lab door. A handful of scientists march through the cement brick corridor outside the lab with their touchpads in hand. Electric lamps, undulating from an unseen draft, light the bland hallway. Rooms, mostly labs, are spaced evenly apart. Chase ignores his colleagues as he heads for the elevator at the end of the corridor. They all ignore each other. It is rather unprofessional to do otherwise. Given a mission, they must always remain focused. To be unfocused would be a threat to their entire operation.

On the top floor, Dr. Morey's office looks over bleak Orbis City, or Orbis for short. The Orbis Institute, where Dr. Morey and Chase both work, was erected in the center of the city centuries ago before everything fell apart after the 2250 Cyber Panic. Orbis, by all known records, is the only surviving human colony. All others have perished. Rumor has it that a paradise of sort lies beyond the massive half-a-mile high wall surrounding Orbis, but rumors shall always remain rumors. Weeding out conspiracy theories is like weeding out the possibility unicorns may exist. It's silly and beyond empirical study.

Standing an incredible seven feet tall, Dr. Morey wears a diplomatic smile wherever he goes. It's not necessarily appealing; instead, it always seems to play coy with his real intentions. Nonetheless, no one interrogates a 270-pound man who runs the most extensive scientific research center known to exist. Shaking his hand, Chase takes a seat in front of Dr. Morey's antique mahogany desk. It is one of the few remnants from the past that remains in mint condition. Many others are broken, worthless, or are rotting in a museum hardly visited by Orbis's citizens. History is a sore subject.

"Dr. Hartford," Dr. Morey booms, his voice carrying across the entire floor, "I'm glad you came to see me so quickly."

"It is my duty, is it not?" Chase replies, resting his slender hands on his lap.

"It is only a part of your duty. Only a part. A part that fits a much grander mission."

"Yes, sir."

Meddling with his pocket watch chain strung across his suit jacket, Dr. Morey leans back in his leather chair. The chandelier suspended above him shines on his round visage.

"I supposed you are curious why I have called you up here," he says, not bothering to look at Chase.

"Most certainly. Anything that invokes you to interrupt my studies tends to gain my attention."

"You have always been astute. That is why I like you so much, Dr. Hartford. That is also why I have set you in charge of our most delicate project. The Sigmund Project."

"Much appreciated, sir."

Smiling, Dr. Morey stands to his feet. Hands in his pockets, he meanders towards the window overlooking the city.

"Please join me, Dr. Hartford." Chase complies, keeping his back straight as he stands a perfect arm's length away from Dr. Morey who asks, "What do you see?"

"I observe there to be thousands of buildings, many structurally insecure, constantly under renovation. A million bustling bodies attending to the day's work ahead.

A vastly bland world. That, of course, is my very own conjecture."

"Of course," Dr. Morey says with a nod, "those are accurate statements. I fear far too accurate. Have you heard yet about the bombing that occurred on Twelfth Street? It happened in the Lockhaven sector."

"I have heard bits and pieces through my tube at home, but nothing very detailed."

"Another radical. Some drunkard who wanted to get a reaction from us."

"The authorities took care of it, I presume."

"Of course. Of course. A cleanup crew swept the area, washed the blood, and followed common protocol."

"Is that why you called me to your office?"

Looking at Chase grimly, Dr. Morey grunts, "Partially. There has been a rise in tension lately. Not many are radicals per se, but there is a certain inkling of doubt regarding our practices here."

Frowning, Chase shakes his head, "I thought most still trust us or, at the very least, are indifferent."

"Most still do, of course. The majority can always be swayed, however, if vexed enough."

"Certainly."

Turning on his heels, Dr. Morey stares into Chase's beady eyes. Resting a heavy hand on Chase's shoulder, Dr. Morey gives it a good squeeze.

"I am counting on you, Dr. Hartford, to accomplish what we are attempting to do here. Do remember, our mission is to use our resources to create a pragmatic world. A place where people can stop worrying about meaningless things. I trust that you have made progress."

Returning Dr. Morey's fixed gaze, Chase nods, "I am. It is very challenging, but with time, I will certainly accomplish the goal at hand."

Smiling, Dr. Morey pats Chase on the cheek, "That is all I wanted to hear from you. You will give the people what they need. Orbis will be set right once again."

***

Chase roves through the Paddington sector just outside the Orbis Institute's main gate on his way home. His home, only a fifteen-minute walk from Orbis Institute's security gate, rests peacefully in the nicer part of the city. Most people who work for Orbis Institute live in Paddington or Barrington. They are the wealthiest sectors out of the six that circle the city. Paddington had the unfair advantage of being built near the main water spring. Flocking there, those with money or power speedily made settlement. Barrington just accumulated wealth over time because the largest construction company was founded there a little over fifty years ago.

Brushing Chase's leg, a scrap of newspaper flutters by. The headline, with a provocative picture, exclaims, "SHOOTING IN HASPOCK KILLS THREE." Chase swallows the memory welling up inside his throat. During his time pursuing a master's degree in chemistry and physics, he got a call that rocked his world. While driving to Barrington to scout out a small apartment complex for sale, Chase's parents got caught in the middle of a shoot-out. Shattered into pieces, their skulls littered the inside of their beautiful Rolls Royce handcrafted before the panic. His friends, very few in number, told him to take time to grieve. He couldn't. Chase stuck up his lip, accepted the fact that the world is cold, and pressed harder into his studies. Mourning was painful and a waste of valuable time. He may have lost everyone who was ever close to him that horrid day, but his position at Orbis wouldn't have been possible without it.

Arriving at his Mediterranean-style house nestled in a quiet development fenced off from the rest of the city, Chase kicks his shoes off inside. Peering through his window like a peeping tom, the moon stalks Chase's footsteps across his wooden tiling. The stars, filling the sable sky like a celestial army, light his path. Grabbing a beer from his titanium alloy fridge, he plops down on a soft recliner, a relic from the past that Chase delights in the most. Switching on his tube, black and white fuzz zig zags across the screen. A red triangle flashes on the screen with "WAIT" in its center. After a few minutes, the tube goes black, then a click sound activates the daily broadcast.

"I'm Samantha Pierce. As you can see, the clean-up crews cleared the debris from yesterday's bombing on Twelfth Street," a beautiful, blond-haired woman reports. "According to witnesses, the radical drove a brown pick-up truck loaded with explosives into what used to be a small pizza joint." Behind Samantha, black and yellow caution tape seals off the remaining char that coats the concrete ground. A couple of people in fluorescent vests investigate for evidence. Samantha continues, "Officials said that the man was intoxicated and was intending to ram the Orbis Institute's protective wall."

"Even that many explosives would have barely put a dent into our wall," Chase comments to himself, taking a swig from his drink. The Orbis Institute, intuitively engineered, is a state-of-the-art facility. Granted, the lights can be finicky, but that has more to do with external problems. Blackouts are not uncommon in Orbis. Understaffed, the power center runs about as smoothly as a square tire. Otherwise, Orbis Institute is indisputably a work of genius. Its founder, Christian Worthington, erected the institute on a modified cement platform made from a sophisticated diamond solution. Standing thirty-five stories tall, it wasn't always the tallest building, but today it is. A reinforced steel wall guards it against outside threats. However, what is most intriguing about the institute is the tunnel system. Dozens of tunnels stretch across Orbis City, unbeknownst to most of its citizens. They are only accessible to and known, for that matter, by a handful of Orbis Institute workers. Chase is one of them.

When Christian built the institute, he intended for it to revolutionize the world. A dream unfolded before him like a beautiful fairy tale. Singing, dancing, rejoicing, people across the world were going to be in perfect bliss because of Orbis. The city was built, and everything seemed like it was going to Christian's plan until the year

2250 arrived; then everything went to crap. For unknown reasons, Christian's board of directors evicted him and set a new man in charge by the name of Adam Gray. It didn't take long for Adam to exploit Orbis's resources, creating worldwide panic. Details are blurry, mostly because everyone experienced the panic differently, but what is important is that over three-quarters of the world died in a matter of weeks. Those who survived either suffered from radiation, disease, or weird artificial intelligence parasites Adam accidentally released. Some survivors clawed their way to Orbis. All others have been assumed dead. No one can live beyond the walls.

Adam built the massive wall that surrounds the city practically overnight. He knew it would be the only way they'd survive. Declining in morale, Orbis's biggest threat was internal conflict. Riots broke out, and people across the sectors rose in arms against Orbis Institute. Years of the conflict nearly led to the absolute decimation of humanity until Dr. Morey's great-great-grandfather took over. He brutally cracked the whip, set everyone straight, and began to focus on internal repair. The city is far from a utopia, but it is stable for now. That, in a sense, is the goal of Orbis. That is Chase's mission. To make Orbis into a utopia just as Christian envisioned.

As Chase sits watching Samantha babble about useless city affairs, his mind is elsewhere. He is continually thinking about the mission at hand. Internalizing it, it never leaves his head. Orbis City is astronomically unaware of how sophisticated Chase's study is. If they were aware, everything would go to hell.

Chapter 2

At 6 a.m. sharp, Chase leaves his house. Peeking over the horizon, the sun greets Orbis with an inauspicious glow. Mumbling data to himself, he walks through the empty streets. Five minutes from Orbis Institute, he glances at the outskirts of Boltstock, the sector right beside Paddington. Deteriorating, the concrete establishments ranging from apartments to shady barber shops scream poverty. The streets, littered with cigarette butts, beer cans, used condoms, and other mystery items, Chase wouldn't even think about getting near, wait anxiously for the day ahead. Plastered on one of the walls, a banner lettered with red spray paint demands the attention of any passerby:

WHAT THE HELL ORBIS?!

Sighing, Chase averts his eyes from the obscene sign. Muttering further data, he scrunches his eyebrows.

"Sample 287 responded well to solution Charlie Three. I may need to run a few tests on different colored samples to make sure there is no difference in results. I doubt there to be any sort of change."

"Hey!" a haggard voice calls.

Stopping, Chase turns around. A wiry fellow with splotchy skin that looks cancerous stands half a block away. Shaking violently, the man points a bloody finger at Chase's heart like a dagger. Holding back tears, he grinds his molars with a sort of tenacity only found in the mentally deranged. Clothes, filthy rags patched together hang from his dirty body.

"What do you want?" Chase asks, keeping his distance.

"Do you work for the institute?"

"Yes."

"Don't screw up. We're trusting you," the man says as he sniffles and wipes his nose. Fresh blood trickles down his cheek. Dabbing his dilated eyes, he fights a quiver troubling his bottom lip. Looking back at Chase, the man whispers, "I'm trusting you. We all are." Cursing, he runs off behind a shabby apartment complex.

With his hand pressed against his side, Chase lets out a sigh. Tickling his face, a breeze sweeps through the street.

"Maybe we made a mistake," he mumbles to himself.

***

"Break off another sample for me," Chase says. The thud of a hammer reverberates off the walls.

Titus Simmons, Chase's colleague, funnels a pinch of white powder into a clear test tube. Handing the vial to Chase, Titus places the remaining sample inside freezer 325. A crimson solution sits idly in a flask resting on the corner of Chase's desk. Chase's black pupils scrutinize the fluid. Pouring the white powder into the crimson liquid, he watches the dust dissolve like melting snow. Bubbles race to the top of the flask. Hastily grabbing a nearby cork, Titus plugs the vial. Drops of fluid run down the outside of the flask, embracing freedom.

"That was close," Titus mutters, grabbing paper towels beneath the table. Wiping the mess, he gently pushes the vial to the side.

"I never saw it bubble like that before," Chase whispers, leaning in closer, "maybe we're on to something. What sample was that?"

"325," Titus says. Clearing his throat, he scratches the back of his head. Glancing at the freezers, he whispers, "Does it bother you—"

"Silence. 325. Sample 325. Sample 325 is very tender." Picking up his notes, Chase hastily flips through pages before reaching a yellow sheet with the number 325 in the corner. "Sample 325 is from Africa. A heavy specimen, all things considered." Mumbling, Chase's dark eyes dart across the scribbles like they are holy words. Random grunts proceed from his lips, causing Titus to raise his eyebrow.

"Dr. Hartford, with all due respect, I believe using a touchpad would be more effective," Titus says.

"I'd much rather express my thoughts on paper than on a screen. It promotes brain activity. Perhaps you could use some," Chase replies coldly. "You interrupted me, Titus."

"Dr. Simmons," Titus mumbles under his breath.

"You're Titus to me."

"Just because you're the head of Dr. Morey's wonder project doesn't give you the right to disrespect me."

Standing up straight, Chase raises his sharp chin at Titus's forehead. Shame washes over Titus's face, flushing his cheeks.

"Dr. Simmons," Chase says sardonically, "I will have you know that I have been with this institute for over a decade. I spent most of my growing years studying the sciences ranging from chemistry to astronomy. I have a proven genius IQ and can solve nearly any mathematical equation in my head. Your lack of experience, puny degree, and frivolous mind pose no threat. Do you understand?" Titus nods, avoiding Chase's eyes. "Good. Consider yourself dismissed. I will retrieve you if I need your assistance again."

Titus scampers through the lab door like a dog with his tail tucked between his legs. Heaving a sigh, Chase wipes his brow.

"The upcoming scientists don't understand respect," he grumbles to himself, "they make it here thinking they're really something. Fools."

Grabbing the flask, he raises it to his face. The fluid, speckled with green spots resembling algae, has settled. An odd stillness has passed over it. It's an unsettling stillness. Lowering the flask, Chase jots down more notes.

"Green specimens," Chase mutters to himself, completing an entry, "just may be the beginning of life."

***

"Crazy radical claims to be from beyond the wall," Samantha says, standing in front of a SWAT van. "The radical, who goes by the name Oliver, was arrested just moments ago for raising an uproar." A giant, beige-skinned man, holding a foreboding Taser rod, glances over at Samantha. He stands by the SWAT van with his attention solely on the news anchor. "According to reports, he was speaking out against the Orbis Institute for their 'cruel behavior.' Gaining an audience, he proceeded to speak about life beyond Orbis, but..." Marching towards Samantha, the giant law enforcer with his huge black, bulletproof vest, lowers his Taser by his side.

"Go somewhere else," he booms. His voice is deeper than the Mariana Trench.

"Excuse me, what?" Samantha asks, her arms crossed.

"Get out of here."

"We are reporting—"

"Yeah. And I'm telling you to knock it off. Get the hell out of here."

"You can't—"

Shoving his huge hand into the camera, the giant man curses before a couple of shrieks pierce the air.

Chapter 3

"I assume you heard about that Oliver character," Dr. Morey says, fiddling with his pocket watch. Chase nods. His hands, set professionally by his side, suppress the nervous energy surging through his veins. Snorting, Dr. Morey leans against the cement wall, his finger tapping it with scorn. "All those radicals could go to hell for all I care," he mutters. "We are trying to save humanity, and all they want to do is ruin it."

"Do you think his comment regarding our practices here as cruel has any merit?" Chase asks. His pointer finger twitches. Hiding the frown nagging his lips, he holds his stern complexion.

Pausing until a fellow scientist passes by into another lab, Dr. Morey whispers, "I consider it a cost. Not cruelty. We take one damn thing away from them, with hardly a qualm; now everything is a question. May I remind you that they willingly agreed to this project of ours? Now, as speculation arises, some consider the fact we may be tampering in some sort of injustice. They don't know what is happening here, nor do they truly care. All they want is a future. We'll give them that much."

"I suppose they have reason to trust us as well as a reason to be concerned."

"They trust us, and they are concerned. It's a double-edged sword. They swing one way then the other. At the end of the day, law enforcement will keep those in check who cross the line, and Orbis will hear our loyal supporters."

Clearing his throat, Chase wipes his dry lips with the back of his hand. Scratching his thigh, he says, "Sounds like a well-developed plan. Now, if you excuse me, I must use the lavatory."

"Of course. Please, be on your way. Just remember, Orbis is counting on you, Dr. Hartford. Prove this Oliver character wrong."

Nodding, Chase hurries for the restroom. Quickly floundering through the nearest stall, he locks the portal. In Chase's sweaty palm is a crumpled letter. Flattening it against the wall, he rests it on the tank. Dropping his drawers, he sits down, bringing the letter close to his dark eyes. He was just given the message this morning by Skyler. He was interrupted by Dr. Morey before being able to comprehend what it meant. He asked Skyler who it was from, but she didn't know. It appeared untampered with when he opened it.

Dr. Hartford,

End this cruel project of yours. You do not understand what you are doing. End it now. I will help you.

Oliver

"Cruel project," Chase whispers to himself. A muffled cough proceeds from the other stall. "Cruel project," Chase whispers quieter this time. Fixing his glasses, he reads the small parcel of paper again and again. It's a simple message, but what is bothering Chase is the ending.

Help? How? Chase thinks to himself. *Oliver wound up in prison. If he wants to help anyone, he would not have let himself get arrested. Yet, there must have been something that drove him to do such a thing. Maybe, like the crackhead that stopped me, he is unstable mentally.*

Flushing the toilet, the man in the other stall noisily puts his pants back on. Slamming the stall door behind himself, he whistles as he leaves the restroom.

"Asshole," Chase grumbles. Peering at the letter, he reflects on what Oliver said. He vehemently insisted that he is not from Orbis. Records could prove whether that claim is valid or not. Everyone in Orbis has their DNA recorded in a computer system located in the Orbis Institute's government sector. If his claim regarding his origins is proven false, then whatever gibberish he spewed after that is discredited. However, if he is right about where he came from, that changes how Chase approaches Oliver.

Staring at the stall's door, Chase's eyes furrow. Tucked into his mouth, his cheeks solidify as a sheet of sternness covers his face. He is on the verge of a breakthrough, and he cannot bring the Sigmund Project to a halt. This is his destiny, but he must consider all the facts and validate Oliver's claims. Rising to his feet, Chase fastens his pants. Shoving the note into his pocket, he clears his throat. His usual strict demeanor permeates his body. Straightening his back, he unlocks the portal and marches into the white corridor.

Turning the speakers on, Chase smiles at the sound of "Inventions and Sinfonias." Grabbing his lab coat from the hook by the door, he puts it on over his polo. He snaps his fresh latex gloves against his wrists. Opening freezer 325, he pushes aside the rest of the sample, only interested in the flask. With great precaution, he gently sets it down on his table. Pulling the chair closer, he sits down, eyeing the vial. The green specimens that floated across the top of the solution have now consumed the rest of the fluid. Like a crumpled tissue, the algae-like substance transformed into a flakey, bronze, folded strand of skin.

Pulling tweezers from his lab coat, Chase pulls the skin from the flask like he's performing brain surgery. Hours seem to slip by as his fingers stealthily inch the specimen from its containment. Carefully, ever so carefully, he flattens the skin against the table. Leaning over the new substance, he analyzes it with hawk eyes. Microfibers weave together like a master knitter crafted them. Its durability, greater than Chase's strength, matches that of a bear's. Despite the flakes that flutter onto the table, it remains intact.

Retrieving his notes from the second drawer, he begins to burn a new entry into his records.

Skin. I have made skin.

Sputtering, the vents spit a bout of cold air, sending chills throughout Chase's body. His diabolical smile, revealing each and every tooth, fades. For a second, a frown replaces his pleased disposition. Oliver's words run through his mind.

Chase hates being wrong. The Sigmund Project, although not entirely his own, was predominately his idea. A little over a decade ago, a few years out of school, Chase sat at a meeting with some of the most powerful people in Orbis, Dr. Morey being the greatest of them all. Discussing ways to create a thriving and efficient Orbis, the circular room full of the most brilliant thinkers offered hundreds of plans. Chase's, after some refinement, was the one accepted. That's how, as a young scientist, Chase managed to gain such a lofty position in the institute. He is, after all, a genius.

"Damn radical," Chase whispers to himself. He can't possibly be wrong. Chase calls for Skyler over the intercoms and asks if Harriet is available.

"She is currently in her office," Skyler replies.

"Is she available for a visit?"

A brief pause follows before Skyler says, "Yes."

Taking the elevator to the 20th floor, Chase walks into a circular office. Harriet, a big-boned, red-head with freckles plaguing her face, stands at her computer. Her frame, wider than a tractor-trailer truck, is uncomfortable to fit inside a chair. She'd much rather stand while she works.

"Harriet," Chase chimes, a smirk plastered on his face.

Looking up from her computer, she casts an array of dimples across her plump cheeks.

"Dr. Hartford, what a pleasant surprise," she says, her voice nearly as high as a dog whistle. To many people's dismay, it is audible to human ears.

"How are you doing this fine morning?"

"Can't complain. How about you?"

Chase shrugs, "Another day, another dollar. Harriet, could you, by chance, retrieve a DNA record on a particular figure?"

"Whose file would you like me to find?" Harriet asks, her fingers set over the keyboard.

"I would like to verify whether or not that radical by the name of Oliver can be found in our records."

"Do you have his full name?"

"I'm afraid not."

Frowning, Harriet steps back from her computer. She says, "I can search Oliver, but there may be multiple Olivers. It would be best if I had his DNA sample and could scan our system for his file. That would be the most accurate method."

"Shit," Chase grumbles, "could you accomplish that by the end of the day?"

"Of course. I could get one of our correctional officers to receive the sample. I'm sure he is on record. We have yet to have it any other way."

"Thank you, Harriet."

"Any time. I'll notify Skyler to reach you once the results come in."

Nodding his head, Chase heads for his laboratory until the results arrive.

***

"What are you suggesting, Harriet?" Chase asks, his palms fused by sticky sweat. He leans forward; his chair aches from depending on its two legs too long. Sliding down his nose, his glasses fog from unseen anxiety.

"I can't explain it, Dr. Hartford," Harriet huffs, her red hair frazzled. Flushed, her normally rosy cheeks are pale, highlighting the ugly freckles riddled across her face.

"Are you sure? Are you sure that you did not find him on record?"

"I searched his sample three times, Dr. Hartford. I swear. I swear!" Harriet exclaims, her voice ringing Chase's ears.

"Calm down. Calm down. I believe you."

"This never happened before. I swear."

"I'm sure it hasn't, Harriet. I'm sure."

"What are we supposed to do about this?"

"Create a new entry, like you do after our monthly census, and report to the news that you found his record in our system."

"Why?"

"Do you know how people would react if he weren't on record? Notify Samantha's team that you have updated information regarding Oliver. Create fake data, get creative, and as soon as people believe he is from Orbis, there will be no more talk regarding his authenticity."

Typing like mad, Harriet's fingers are a blur. Preparing a message for Mendacium News, she mouths the words to herself.

"I hope Samantha doesn't try to get her pretty ass in my office and ask a laundry list of questions. I do terrible under pressure."

"Harriet, you are practically a queen. Samantha can only talk to you if you want her to. Relax," Chase says, shaking loose the pins and needles in his fingers.

"You're right. You're right," Harriet breaths. Slowing, her fingers settle into a regular typing pace. Finishing her message, she looks at Chase, "What are we going to do about this, though?"

"I'll handle it. Just keep Orbis in the dark."

"Ok. Ok."

"It'll be fine, Harriet. Trust me."

"It'll be fine. It'll be fine," Harriet whispers to herself, her eyes closed.

"It'll be fine," Chase confirms, rising to his feet. *I'll make sure it's fine.*

Chapter 4

Stepping from her shower, Samantha grabs her warm towel draped over her brass towel stand. Wrapping her body in the inviting warmth, she smiles. Her fingers run through the soft fabric. Her slippers, resembling two-toothed bunnies, hug her damp feet. Clearing the fog from her mirror, she dabs at the black and blue spot claiming the real estate beneath her left eye.

"I hope Brad doesn't think too much of it." Brad, one of Samantha's friends with benefits, is the son of Lawrence, a wealthy restaurant owner in downtown Paddington. "Why did that bastard have to ruin my beautiful complexion?" Rubbing the spot some more, she winces. "Shit. Shit."

Reaching for her brush, she stares at the mirror intently. Her eyes, scrutinizing every strand of silky hair, are never satisfied. Pulling her hair back as perfect as can be, she frets over a strand that doesn't seem to suit her wants. "Stupid piece of hair," she mutters. Pulling her towel above her breasts, she meanders to her room. Slipping on a scarlet nightgown, she poses in front of her mirror. Her hips, carved for the very purpose of sexual allure, do not fill her cravings. "Too thin." Just yesterday, they were too fat. Voluptuous, her body grabs the attention of any passerby but lets her criticism run free. Pretending to laugh, she practices for the night. The mirror has watched this show a thousand times over. It has yet to watch her address life as it is.

Returning to her bathroom mirror after an hour, she coats her left eye in concealer to hide the blemishes and flaunt the perceived beauty. Blowing a kiss at the mirror, she smiles despite the cries of unrest in her soul. "Brad won't even notice."

Leaning back on her velvet chaise longue, Samantha picks up her touchpad from the coffee table. A green bubble in the corner of the screen notifies her of one new message.

"From Harriet. What does she want?" Samantha whispers to herself. Then there is a knock on her French doors.

"Shit, it's Brad," she whispers. Combing through her hair with her fingers, she checks the polish on her nails. Wiping the corners of her mouth, she smacks her lips together. Satisfied, she calls him in. Brad, a handsome brunette, steps inside. His hazel eyes, full of lechery, scan the apartment. Rugged, his chest boasts through his V-neck. Chiseled to compete with angels, his legs are unashamed to brag strength through his slim jeans.

"Sam, oh Sam," he says. His voice is oily. His fluffy hair bounces with his every step.

"Just give me a minute, Brad," Samantha says as she skims Harriet's message.

"A minute? I don't think I can wait for a second," Brad whispers as he straddles Samantha. Laying on her gently, he caresses her neck.

"Brad knock it off," she giggles. "A lead. Oliver is a fake."

"Just agree to whatever the silly message says and get on with tonight," Brad whispers.

"Fine. Fine. Yes. Oliver is a fake. Screw it." Setting her touchpad on the coffee table, Samantha kisses Brad back, reaching beneath his shirt.

***

"According to newly found evidence, Oliver is in fact from Orbis," Samantha reports outside Orbis Institute,

"His DNA record was discovered by Harriet Walsh the government sector's president."

Turning the tube off, Dr. Morey leans back in his office chair. The tube, staring at him from the corner of the room, hides behind a veil of static before fading into a black abyss. Chortling to himself, he walks over to the window. Gazing at Orbis, he watches the streets bustle with busybodies. No play. Only work. How fruitless their toil is? They build only for buildings to collapse again.

It can be rather demoralizing. Hopefully, the project at hand will eliminate that issue. Hopefully, it will eliminate all problems.

***

Wearing large, circular glasses two shades too dark, Chase wanders through Orbis's finest prison, Lockhaven Confound. A security guard named Pablo, a short Hispanic man with a lisp whenever he pronounces words with the letter "S," leads Chase down a narrow corridor. On each side of them are several cells enclosed by concrete bricks and steel. Each cell has a small window where food passes through, and prison wardens strike necessary conversations. Mumbling, prisoners lounge on their beds, sit in lonely corners, or do pushups to keep themselves entertained. They pay little attention to Chase, who looks odder than they do.

"You got about fifteen minutes with the guy before I gotta get you out," the security guard says with a throat full of saliva.

"Thank you," Chase replies, ignoring the spittle hanging from the guy's mouth. Spitting a wad of chew into a nearby trash can, the security guard pulls out a keycard. Running it by a red laser, cell 77 opens. Inside, on his knees, Oliver rests by his bed with his eyes towards heaven.

"He's all yours," Pablo mutters, locking the cell door behind Chase.

"Great," he mutters.

Rising from his transfixed state, Oliver sits on the end of his bed, facing Chase. His eyes, ocean blue, could set any troubled heart at ease. Smooth, his olive skin soaks in the light hanging from the center of the cell. Carrying an odd aura of boldness with him, Oliver seems rather poised for being locked up only a day ago.

"So, you are Oliver?" Chase asks, leaning back against the cell door.

"As you say, such am I," Oliver replies. His gentle voice doesn't waiver. It is steady and smooth.

"Oliver, I have a few questions for you. Since I have a limited amount of time to spend here, I must not dawdle."

"Perfectly understood. I'm sure anyone with your position would feel entitled to have any question they have answered."

"Someone in my position?"

"Is that one of your few questions?"

"Do you know who I am?"

"I sent you a letter, didn't I?"

"Of course. Of course. How do you know me?"

Smirking, Oliver rubs his thumb against his palm. "When you live beyond the walls, you begin to see the world in a whole new light. I know much more than you could imagine."

"How did you get through the wall?"

"Why would you like to know? In order to fill the hole?"

"Possibly, but I would like to verify your bold claims."

"You didn't find my DNA, did you?"

Cleaning his glasses, Chase sighs, "No. You are the only person without any DNA record."

Smirking, Oliver scuffles to the head of his bed. Sitting up straight, he shakes his head, "You'll get a shock when you try to read my DNA. I'm sure of it."

"What are you? An alien? Trust me, you may be from beyond the wall, but there's a logical reason."

"I do not deny that, but when you discover that your logic and true logic differ, I will be here waiting."

"I always despised those who were arrogant for no good reason."

"Forgive me if I come across as arrogant, but insight and arrogance are two different entities," Oliver says, clasping his hands together. "Beyond the wall, you are correct to assume there are miles of dreadful waste. Mankind did not treat Earth well, I fear."

"Great—"

"I'm not done," Oliver states sternly, "I said you are correct to assume there are miles of dreadful waste. You were incorrect to assume that was it. There is life. Life beyond Orbis."

Raising an eyebrow, Chase's dark eyes look Oliver up and down. He appears, by all observable features, human. Yet, Chase can't shake the looming presence that Oliver emits. It's supernatural.

"Is this colony of life where you are from?" Chase asks, not sure if he can trust Oliver.

"Colony? That's a word for it. In one regard, yes, that is where I am from. However, that *colony* doesn't limit me as you think."

"Who are you? Just tell me," Chase sneers, "I had a list of deductive questions, but they seem quite irrelevant at this point. Just give me a brief synopsis of your life, interest in Orbis, and why Orbis's mission is cruel."

"A brief synopsis," Oliver chuckles. "I can tell that you are a scientist. Has it ever occurred to you that life may not be as easily stratified as you would like to think? Wouldn't life, the world, and all our questions be so simple if the scientific method could properly address everything? It would be so terribly simple that life would be nothing more than a mathematical equation devoid of beauty."

"Look, I don't give a shit about beauty. I am a professional whose mission is to discover how to prevent Orbis from decaying. Our people are declining in morale, work ethic and are hopelessly self-destructive. I am the solution."

Frowning, Oliver runs his hand through his thick, dark brown hair. Pacing the floor, he mouths a few words to himself before facing Chase.

"My father was the founder of Orbis," Oliver says.

"Liar," Chase growls, "That was several hundred years ago. It's not possible."

Blinking, Oliver stares at Chase. He says, "I said earlier your logic and true logic might not align. I didn't say whether my origin is possible by the way you understand the world. I said what is true."

"How am *I* supposed to believe you if I have no reason to?"

"Are you from beyond the wall? Why do you have the upper hand regarding matters outside your limited world view?"

"You have yet to prove that you are from beyond the wall."

"You can spend your entire life ignoring the evidence — my DNA record, witness testimonies, and my story's consistency — but it will do you no good."

Muttering curse words, Chase massages the bridge of his nose. "Fine. Go on."

Smiling, Oliver continues, "As I said, my father founded Orbis. Christian, in his brilliant wisdom, created a magnificent dwelling. I'm sure you would agree."

"It was revolutionary."

Nodding, Oliver says, "Of course Adam, Christian's HR manager, ended up betraying his trust. It was at that moment that Orbis declined."

"The whole world declined."

"Of course. You should expect that anybody's heart, including Earth, will either sustain or kill the body. However, you assumed that Christian perished, as would most people. Christian is nothing like people."

Checking his watch, Chase frowns. Less than five minutes left. He is chasing fairy tales.

"Christian—"

"Stop," Chase growls. "Enough. I hate wasting time. This was a mistake."

Propping his foot against the wall, Oliver says, "You'll be back. With time."

"In your dreams, maybe."

"Those specimens, as you call them, are far too valuable," Oliver states as if entering an unheard conversation.

"Excuse me?"

"My purpose, my reason for being here, is to prevent you from accomplishing this dreadful mission of yours. I know you truly believe that you are the solution. You're not. I know a better way. It's beyond the walls. It's where I live. You must end this treachery. You are destroying humanity."

"What do you know about what I'm doing?"

"I know you're trying to harden the hearts of everyone so they no longer feel a thing. You're making machines. You're not making a solution."

"Time's up," Pablo states, unlocking the cell door.

"Nice chat," Chase says sarcastically, leaving a tear-filled Oliver.

"Return to me sooner than later!" Oliver cries.

"Lunatic," Chase grumbles.

Chapter 5

Staring at his ceiling, caught in a formidable cloud of confusion, Chase curses beneath his breath. Heartless, the stars mock him. They flaunt their freedom like empyrean gods. Biting his nails, Chase feels the sweat bead around his brow.

He never observed the wasteland beyond the wall. For most of his life, he accepted the previous observations committed to text by scientists. He never questioned their claims. As a teenager, he spent his time reading. While others ran off to test their new hormonal fantasies with their peers, he remembers standing before the gigantic wall surrounding Orbis. Standing before it, feeling rather insignificant, he used to imagine the incredible horrors on the other side. The books he read spoke about parasites, monsters, toxic water, and nuclear waste. Yet, he never studied what they claimed. He never breached the wall. He never interviewed survivors or analyzed the relics retrieved by scavengers.

Now, in prison, sleeps a man who claims to be beyond the wall, a man who, by all known evidence, has no reason to be disregarded. Yet, Chase refuses to embrace him. There are far too many variables at play. Besides, if he were to believe Oliver, his whole world view would have to be readjusted. Years of seemingly robust knowledge decimated by one man. However, to be true to his scientific roots, he cannot ignore the newly discovered evidence.

Scratching his head, Chase mutters beneath his breath, "Dammit."

Smash!

Glass shatters downstairs as a thud strikes the wall.

"What is going on?" Chase grumbles, peering over his blanket. Darkness covers his eyes. Fumbling with his glasses on the nightstand, Chase quietly stands to his feet. Obnoxious door slamming follows another shattered window. Tiptoeing across his carpeted room, Chase dunks his hand into a fishless tank. Beneath the rainbow-colored pebbles is a plastic bag. Pulling it out, he opens the bag drawing a black pistol. He had it ever since his parents died.

Wiping his palms, partially wet from the tank and partially from sweat, against his sweatpants, he slinks downstairs. The stairs, scared out of their wits, sit still like stumps, not making a noise. The walls, terrified, listen to the door bellow. Cocking his gun, Chase aims it at his door. His fingers quiver. His dark eyes focus.

Yelling unbridled, the trespasser continues to beat the door. Cautiously, Chase edges forward. A crack rips through the door. Chase freezes. Grunting, the trespasser, smattered with blood, bursts through the door, surrounded by an explosion of splinters. His naked body quakes. His uncontrolled breathing racks his whole body. His dilated eyes, given a spotlight by the moon, burn with acidic tears. Blood gushes from his nose, lathering his lips. Standing before Chase is the crackhead from a few days ago.

"I can't do it! I can't do it!" the crackhead screams; his vocal cords are on the verge of snapping. Sprinting for the kitchen, he swings open the door rummaging through the shelves. Dumbstruck, Chase remains frozen. He gawks at the unearthly sight distorted by the inky blackness.

"What are you doing in my house?" Chase asks, crushing a shard of glass beneath his big toe. "Shit."

Perking, the crackhead throws a glass of milk onto the floor. The frothy fluid bubbles between his toes.

"You damn monster," the crackhead mutters. "Asshole! You did this! You did this! You did this to me!" Screaming belligerently, blood vessels split his dry skin, and blood rolls down his rigid neck. Punching the wall, his knuckles shatter beneath the impact. "You're in my head! I can't get you out of my head! You took everything from me!" He weeps. His chest, running faster than a racehorse, threatens to pop.

Regaining his sense, Chase points his pistol at the crackhead's heart.

"I did no such thing," Chase replies, his voice endeavoring to remain steady.

"What are you doing in that monstrous building? What are you doing? Oh, god, I can hear screaming. I can hear screaming. Oh god. Get it out of there! Get it out of there!" Punching his skull, the crackhead shrieks. Blood sputters from his mouth. "They're under my skin. I can feel it. Every last one of them! Dammit!" Scratching his skin raw, he writhes on the floor. Balling, he cuts his chest with a piece of serrated glass.

"I hear her. I hear weeping. I hear her crying for help. Merry freedom!" Looking at Chase, the crackhead growls, "I see you. You damn hellion!" Screaming bloody murder, the crackhead charges Chase with the piece of glass in hand. Pooling around his trembling fingers, blood pours across his white hand.

Firing two quick shots, Chase swears. Collapsing to his knees, the crackhead falls face-first into his piece of glass, impaling his eye. Chase readjusts his glasses. He closes his eyes for a second to calm his breathing as the stars watch, amused. Garnishing the crackhead with silver light, the moon highlights Chase's adversary.

"I need to call Dr. Morey."

***

"We discarded the body," Dr. Morey whispers, leaning over his desk, "and your windows will be replaced by the time you get home."

"Thank you," Chase sighs. Frowning, Dr. Morey sits back in his chair. Black circles wrap around his wide eyes.

"Must have been terribly frightful. Did this belligerent intruder have any obvious motive, or was he simply psychotic?"

"It would appear that our Sigmund Project may have affected him."

"Yes, I had Harriet find his file for us. Axel Blade Friedman. A poor name choice if you ask me," Dr. Morey grunts. "He was a single father. His wife died a couple of years ago, and his daughter is eleven. He has no known criminal record, although it would appear his drug addiction got the best of him."

"I don't believe the drugs incited his rage, but rather aggravated it."

"What do you mean?"

"As I said, I believe he had a motive for targeting my place. He had a personal vendetta set against me because I am the head of our primary project here at Orbis Institute."

Grumbling, Dr. Morey swivels in his chair. Rubbing the chain draped across his body, he leans over his desk again.

"Dr. Hartford, for your own protection, I will notify Harriet to surround your home with private guards. Do not, under any circumstances, disclose this to any of your colleagues. I do not trust anyone. The sooner we are able to accomplish our task, the sooner civilization will be free from their destruction."

"Dr. Morey, with all due respect, I fear our project may be too narrow. I have been able to make exponential progress, but the entire ordeal seems rather callous."

"What do you mean?"

Clearing his throat, Chase rubs his mole-infected cheek. Taking a deep breath, he says, "Let us assume that our subjects do evolve the way we intend them to. Which should be possible, do not doubt that. What if, like a mathematical equation, it limits our options. Potentially there is another way."

Gritting his teeth, Dr. Morey paces the floor. He glances at the tube and then at the floor. Swearing under his breath, Dr. Morey causes the floor the rumble with each step he takes. Chase sits still.

"Dr. Hartford," Dr. Morey says between his teeth, "I hope you are not considering the notion of abandoning Sigmund, especially after years of endless work and studying."

"Of course not," Chase replies, his mouth feeling oddly dry, "I am still pursuing our desired goal. I must wonder if there could be another way."

"Dr. Hartford, as you so carelessly compared Sigmund to a mathematical equation, you had a hint of truth in your analogy. Like a mathematical equation, Orbis only has one cure, which is the Sigmund Project. That is what we are striving to solve."

Biting his thin lip, Chase wrestles the ambiguous feeling of guilt. Guilt, a feeling relatively uncommon in Chase's life, carries with it an indescribable weight. Chase never harbored any sentiment towards the Sigmund Project, but since Oliver has breached the wall, he seems to have awakened a pernicious spirit that was in comatose. A spirit Chase despises. Yet, he knows he should be experiencing it. Uncomfortable, Chase readjusts himself.

"Dr. Hartford," Dr. Morey booms.

"Yes," Chase replies, breaking free from his introspective trance.

"Can I trust you?"

"Of course," Chase says, "Of course. The Sigmund Project has my full commitment."

"Good," Dr. Morey says, "Good."

Leaving Dr. Morey's office, Chase proceeds downstairs. Oscillating, the lamps dance to the vents' whimsical song of horror. Flickering, their dim luminosity concocts a shadowy revolution. The shadows, however, are far too timid to raise any sort of tumult. Passing through a silent insurgence, Chase stays alert. His ears, inclined to the slightest rustle, intently listen. His eyes, strained by anticipation, look this way and that way. They do not cease to move. Weaving his way through several corridors, he eventually arrives at a metal door clearly labeled for those with platinum IDs. Chase has a platinum ID.

Swiping his card, Chase steps inside another elevator. Closing, the sliding doors lurch the cab. Chase, after clearing his scratchy throat, presses the "B" button. Twiddling his thumbs, he muses over what he should do. Oliver, distinctly seared into his mind, will not let up. He seems to be endlessly speaking, almost like Chase never left the prison. He's still there, with Oliver, enclosed by cement walls, steel, and an impenetrable door.

Coming to a jerky halt, the elevator opens. Green lights on each side of an arched corridor inform Chase's feet where to step. Slate gray concrete, forming the arched passageways, structures the tunnel system beneath Orbis. Hurrying, Chase hustles through numerous pathways before arriving at his destination. A green light positioned above the white lettering illuminates Chase's desired room: Animal Enclosure.

Having few friends, if any at all, Chase developed an interest in animals. A keenness would suggest he liked animals. It was never that way. Instead, he enjoyed toying with the little beasts he owned. Humans, in their natural state, are impossible to control — they're annoyingly complex. Brutes, on the other hand, are relatively dumb. They're easily manipulated and domineered, and they never revolt. Playing king, Chase would treat his animal subjects like slaves. He'd beat them, starve them, and force them to do tricks until they died. Then he bought more so he could always be in control. Like a terrible fiend, life may rob people of power, but humans must do their best to steal it back. One cosmic tyrant versus a million tiny tyrants.

Meandering past the dozens of empty glass enclosures inside Animal Enclosure, Chase focuses on the two pens still in use. The animals, of little help to the Orbis Institute, have been exterminated. If the institute is ever in need of animals again, there are plenty of rats razing the littered streets. People can't slaughter them quick enough. However, for Chase's sake, the institute kept two pens occupied. One, sitting on a black counter, contains sickly rats. The other, positioned beside the table on the floor, includes a hissing bobcat. Towering over the two cages like a sinister god, Chase smirks. His glasses, struck by a stroke of light, gleam, disguising the villainous look in his eyes.

Reaching into a shelf beneath the rat enclosure, Chase conceals something inside his right hand. In the other hand, he holds a slice of moldy bread. Connected to the rat enclosure is a cylinder passageway closed off by a gate. The tiny tunnel has breathing holes on top of the tube. Raising the gate, Chase drops a bread crumb into the cylinder tunnel. Curious, a dirty rat with musty straw stuck to its coarse fur nibbles at the bread. Chase closes the gate silently. Dropping another crumb a little farther ahead, Chase goads the dense rat forward. Trusting the moldy manna giver, the rat's beady eyes lust after another morsel. Then another. Then another. Grinning, Chase drops another piece. Wising up for a second, the rat stops. A scent in the air gives it pause. Sniffing, it stares into the heavens until another scent, far more appealing than danger, grabs its attention. Digging its ugly nose into the final crumb, the rat eats away at the bread. Chase opens a trap door atop the last portion of the tunnel. With his right hand, he shoves the rat into an odious drop using the blunt end of a rod.

Scattering sticks, the rat's plump body arouses the bobcat curled in an ominous corner. Pouncing, before the rat knew where it landed, the bobcat tears the rat to shreds. The rat, shrieking, squeaks hopelessly. It kicks, but nothing in its power can save it. Tearing the fur from its flesh, the bobcat ravages the pitiful creature. Gorging on it like a demon devouring a damned soul, the bobcat purrs gutturally with sadistic pleasure. The living rats, in their tiny enclosure, blithely stare at Chase, oblivious to his treachery. He is just the man with moldy bread.

"Your turn will come. It will come," Chase assures the rats. Looking down at the bobcat's enclosure, Chase watches the beast leave behind a pile of bones, nothing more than an incomplete skeleton. Chase's smile vanishes with a pang of guilt. Grunting, he leaves the room. Locking the door, he glances at the place beside Animal Enclosure. He frowns at the room's title: Dismemberment. Hiding his face, Chase walks away, leaving behind the rooms he sincerely hoped to confront but couldn't. Not right now.

Chapter 6

"You decided to come back, I see," Oliver says with a quirky grin.

"Tell me more about yourself," Chase says, ignoring Oliver's statement.

With his hands folded behind his head, Oliver sits against the wall. He taps his bare foot against the concrete floor. Yet, he doesn't say a word.

"Well, I'm waiting," Chase urges, already annoyed. He has been unable to sleep since he last visited Oliver. All Chase can think about is what Oliver said regarding the Sigmund Project. Triturating his conscious, like an irritating wine press, Oliver's words just grate him. Chase can't do his job the same. He can't do anything the same.

"How is the Sigmund Project coming along?" Oliver asks.

"Why don't you ever answer my questions?"

"Why do you think you ask the right questions?"

"I hate you."

Chuckling to himself, Oliver moves closer to Chase. Sitting on the edge of his bed, Oliver leans on his hands.

"Well, how is it coming along?" Oliver reiterates his question.

"We have made great progress," Chase hisses. "We should have a prototype within the week."

"Yes, a prototype."

"How does that make you feel? Does it make you quiver? We're going to accomplish this cruel project as you rot in jail," Chase sneers. He doesn't approve of the

Sigmund Project like he once did, but his anger towards Oliver supersedes his true beliefs.

Not missing a beat, Oliver retorts, "Who says you are going to accomplish your goal?"

"Didn't I just say we have a prototype on the way? It is only a matter of time."

"You may be able to create a prototype. You may even get as far as having everything you need to accomplish your task, but you will never accomplish your goal."

"What is our goal exactly?" Chase challenges. Removing his glasses, he wipes the mildew from his eyes. He really hasn't been sleeping well.

"Have you been working this hard without a goal?"

"I know our damn goal, but if you know it so well, I would like you to enlighten me."

Not responding, Oliver looks towards the door. Smiling, he returns his gaze to Chase. Beet red, Chase seethes beneath his ugly face.

"Oliver, you are wearing away at my patience. Is your goal to anger me?"

"It isn't to make you happy. Not at least in the way you imagine."

"Ass," Chase mutters, standing to his feet. Pulling at his already thin hair, Chase snaps his head around like a possessed doll. "What do you want from me?"

"I have made that quite clear, but I fear you won't heed to my command unless you trust me. You have yet to trust me," Oliver says, seemingly unphased by Chase's heated demeanor.

"Why should I trust you? You haven't given me a good reason to trust you!"

"Did you test my DNA?"

"See! This is what I'm talking about!" Chase fumes, "I can't get anywhere with you! All you do is ask questions. Why do you ask so many questions?"

"Did you?"

"Yes, you prick. We did."

"Discover anything stunning? Marvelous? Supernatural by chance?"

Grinding his molars, Chase huffs, "Your DNA is unique."

"How?"

Biting his dusty lip, Chase slows his breathing to reply, "It seems to contain every person's recorded DNA but is distinctive by its own means. Almost like a father gene of sorts."

"That is peculiar," Oliver comments, unable to suppress a slight grin. His tan skin seems to glow ever so slightly. Clearing his eyes, Chase assures himself he is hallucinating.

"What game are you playing?" Chase asks. His typical professionalism is crumbling. It started crumbling the moment he stepped into the cell. "Why don't you just tell me who or what you are?" He pleads.

"I am Oliver. I am from beyond the wall. My father is Christian. He lives by an oasis where I came from. That, Chase, is the answer. That is the only place your goal can truly be fulfilled."

Massaging his temples, Chase shakes his air-filled head. He's too tired for this. Yawning, he repositions his glasses. "Are you trying to convince me that these nonsensical claims are true?"

"And you wonder why I ask so many questions."

"What's that supposed to mean?"

"I tell you the truth, but when I tell you the truth, you don't believe it. I don't ask questions for information. If you were curious, I ask questions so that you may discover what is true. You won't believe me because your ears are closed, but with enough prodding, they can be opened."

"You talk like a damn rabbi or something."

Oliver laughs. "I supposed I may."

Sitting down by the cell door, Chase sighs. "You mentioned an oasis. How is that the answer?"

"The oasis itself is not the answer. My father, who lives by the oasis, is."

"How so?"

"He gives freedom."

Groaning, Chase kicks the bed. "Can you be more specific?"

"Specific? I can get more detailed, but that only muddles the truth. He gives freedom," Oliver says.

"Great."

"What is your goal? You never stated what your goal was."

Furrowing his eyebrows, Chase retorts, "Go to hell. I have no reason to tell you anything."

"I suppose," Oliver sighs, "but it is only a matter of time before your actions and their consequences catch up to you. When they do, I expect another visit."

"What consequences?"

"Have you ever stared into their eyes?"

"The subjects?"

"When you do, you'll see me. It'll make your blood run cold and your fingertips numb. Fear, my fear, will run through you like electricity."

Locked in Oliver's gaze, Chase's skin turns to gooseflesh. An icy chill, like a squall from Antarctica, streams down his spine. For a brief second, utter terror sweeps over him just from looking into Oliver's calm, glacier blue eyes.

"Your time's up, pal," Pablo mumbles, unlocking the door.

"Until next time," Oliver says.

"What the hell?" Chase utters, dumbfounded.

"No. Not me."

***

"I'm Samantha Pierce covering what may be the biggest breakthrough in history," Samantha says to a wide-mouthed camera. "According to Dr. Morey, the president of Orbis Institute, his team is on the edge of completing their Sigmund Project."

Sitting at home, millions of people watch their tubes. Some grunt, others retain their ceaseless doubts, but most heave a sigh of relief.

"A prototype may be released for testing within the week."

Watching her tube, Jarita, an Indian woman, relaxes. The ever-increasing wrinkles in her face stretch. Her one-year-old son, Raj, sleeps soundly in his warped crib. Jarita's apartment, a dark cube divorced from the rest of the world, hums. Her fans, rigged with chains around the hubs, rattle. Speakers placed near windows play heavy rock from an ancient mp3 player, a relic she stole from the museum. Her door is barred for war, locked shut by three bolts, a plank, and a padlock.

Blackened by tar, Jarita's fingers fall still. For once, she is still. Closing her eyes, she takes a deep breath. She hears a rustle. Her son gently yawns as he repositions himself beneath a thin blanket. A green polka dot pacifier sits in his mouth. Smiling, Jarita whispers, "I love you, Raj." Heading for the kitchen, she finds her pack of cigarettes inside the top cupboard, just behind her homemade applesauce. Finishing her last box, she curses under her breath. Her kitchen window, like the others, is enshrouded by a thick, sable drape.

Pulling out a wad of cash from her pocket, she counts it in her head. She pick-pocketed a man a few floors down. He doesn't need it, at least not like she does.

"Shit. Only 200. I'll need more than that," Jarita mutters. A rustle catches her attention. "Oh, Raj, are you aw—"

Caving, her door groans in agony. It collapses in seconds as the plank splits like a twig.

"SWAT!" An armored enforcer, prepared for a riot, steps over the rubble with a hulking battery ram. Two other enforcers, with slug guns, slip inside the apartment following their armored leader.

"What the hell!" Jarita shrieks, smashing her cigarette into the counter. "What are you doing?"

"Apprehend the child," the armored enforcer thunders behind his bulletproof face mask. Grabbing a knife by her fridge, Jarita yells. Slinging his gun over his shoulder, an enforcer plucks Raj from his crib by the back of his neck. Balling, Raj cries for his mom through terrified tears.

"Shut up, kid!" the enforcer shouts, shaking Raj like a maraca. The enforcer tries to shove the pacifier into Raj's mouth.

"Stop!" Jarita cries, charging the man with her son. Clobbered upside the head, she collapses to the floor, her head pounding. Setting his battering ram down, the armored enforcer draws a silenced pistol.

"I thought they were done!" Jarita cries. "I thought they have a fucking prototype!"

"Shut up."

Raj cries to his mother's deaf ears as the enforcer throws him into the back of a black van.

***

"Don't make me look like a fool," Dr. Morey says, his face stern, "I gave the people a promise."

"A prediction would be a better description," Chase replies.

"In my books, that is as good as a promise. I stay true to my word."

Chase swallows the scorn in his throat. He knows Dr. Morey is far from an honest man. Brilliant, professional, and efficient, but not honest.

"Of course, Dr. Morey."

"You're going to complete that prototype by tomorrow, correct?"

"I intend to."

"Good," Dr. Morey says, leaning back in his chair. "I will notify the psychologists that their research will be put through its first rigorous test."

Squirming in his seat, Chase locks his disgust inside his anxious heart. Chase has been painfully aware of a transcendent spirit. A nagging spirit. It wrenches his heart unpredictably at work. One moment he may be neck-deep in his studies, then the next, he is drowning in raging guilt. Oliver, aggravating Oliver, swims through that tempestuous flood reminding him how cruel this project is. Losing weight, Chase plays with his food more than he eats it. Oliver has shoved a giant wrench into Sigmund's cogs, and he is wreaking havoc in Chase's mind.

"Dr. Hartford," Dr. Morey booms.

"Yes, Dr. Morey," Chase croaks.

"Get to work. I dismissed you. Get your butt down in that lab of yours."

"Yes, sir."

Chapter 7

Sleep-deprived, Chase furiously scurries across his lab floor. A team of fifteen scientists, including Titus, slave away at completing Sigmund's first prototype. Strained, Chase barks like a rabid rottweiler. His eyes are like monstrous black holes. His teeth, barred, grind away at the morale in the room. Raising his voice every five seconds, he forces his colleagues to suppress their urge to cry. Chase may have had too much to drink the other night, but he doesn't care. It's the only way he can numb his consciousness.

"Titus! Get your head out of your ass! I need that solution to be perfect!" Chase hollers, spittle flying from his mouth.

Shivering, Titus nods. He measures a crimson solution, trying his best to stay steady.

"Greta!" Chase shouts across the floor.

A frail lady, no taller than five feet, chokes a whimper. "Yes, Dr. Hartford," she squeaks.

"Don't handle that bone like a second-rate prostitute! Treat it with respect. Gentle. Gentle, I said!"

Inching forward, Greta lowers a femur bone onto a sanitized, stainless steel table. She can feel Chase's glowering eyes burn a hole through her head. His indignation is red hot.

"Dr. Hartford," a well-collected voice calls.

"What?" Chase growls, snapping his head towards the door. Destiny Collins stands by the door, her hand wrapped around an electronic tablet. She holds her head high and keeps her hair pulled back in a perfect bun.

"What do you want, Dr. Collins? Can't you see I'm in the middle of something?" Chase snaps, a little bit milder this time. Scanning the room, Destiny raises an eyebrow.

"I can see you are handling Sigmund very well."

"Oh, get off your high horse. What do you want?"

"You agreed to meet with me today and discuss the neurotic schematics we gathered on subject 325 and what the Psychology Department plans on doing with the completed subjects."

Taking off his glasses, Chase sighs. His colleagues stare at him, waiting to see if he'll leave just for a moment. Aware of their gazes, Chase roars, "Stop staring! Get back to work! I'll be gone for a bit. Titus!"

"Yes, Dr. Hartford?"

"Keep an eye on everything, and don't screw up."

"Yes, Dr. Hartford."

Sitting inside a circular office, complete with a slide projector and four chairs, Chase and Destiny discuss the next step.

"I'm sure you're well aware that the Psychology Department got tasked with the development process," Destiny says, sitting by the projector. Chase nods from the opposite end of the room. Shaking her head, she inserts some slides into the projector's carousel. Flipping to the first slide, she stands. "Allow me to draw your attention to the limbic system," Destiny says, pointing at a diagram of the brain. "It is, when in relationship with the frontal lobe, the soul of a person. The limbic system dictates how people feel, learn, and remember information. The frontal lobe then creates personality, beliefs and helps develop self-awareness."

"I'm well aware of how the brain works," Chase huffs. Frowning, Destiny wonders how a man can be so thoroughly ugly, not only physically but internally as well.

"I'm glad you studied neurology," Destiny replies sarcastically. "This slide highlights our plan."

"A five-step process. Is this an eighth-grade science fair?"

"Dr. Hartford, I am also an accomplished professional. If you could kindly show me some respect, I would appreciate it."

Chase grumbles.

"Now, as I was saying," Destiny says, looking back at the screen, "we plan on targeting these two sections of the brain. And yes, we have a five-step plan. I assure you, I could get very technical, but for the sake of simplicity, I generalized our process."

"Your first step is to create new memories?"

"Yes and no. We will, in a way, give them the same memories. Your prototype, for instance, has all its memories stored in our database. We are prepared to download those when the prototype is ready. However, we will tweak those memories so that it sees them from a new perspective."

"What do you mean, a new perspective?"

"The daydreams, the numerous infatuations with the wasteland on the other side of the wall, will be edited. Instead of seeing possibilities, subject 325, along with the others, will see absolutes. There is nothing beyond the wall. Goals to become something invaluable, such as a philosopher, artist, or musician, will be seen as ridiculous. We are not concerned with transcendence. Orbis is all that really exists and matters."

Biting his tongue, Chase wants to lash out. What is Orbis surviving for? What is it striving for? Why should these specimens care about this enclosed hell hole?

"Then you want to solidify these memories into fundamental beliefs," Chase mutters, gazing at the grainy projection on the wall.

"Exactly. As these subjects age, they will see Orbis as the capital of thought, meaning, and value. They will believe these walls are, as we know, protectors. Instead of feeling the tug for adventure, they will reason that the tug is superstitious in nature. They will believe in Orbis alone."

Chase can feel the bile in his stomach bubble. He feels sick. Whispering in his ear, Oliver pecks at the back of his head.

"Just sum up the rest for me," Chase groans.

"Sure," Destiny says, frowning, "the next steps just follow a logical progression. After the beliefs develop, the Psychology Department will teach these subjects how to view emotions."

"How is that?"

"They will see them as either motivator, if beneficial to their practice, or as obstacles. Of course, some subjects will tend to create emotions into a god, which we won't entirely discourage; it may be good for morale. We will just make sure that the emotions they desire propel Orbis forward."

"Forward," Chase snorts.

"Excuse me?" Destiny questions, her fists on her narrow hips.

"What are we classifying as forward?"

"Technological developments, efficiency, better standards of living."

"Damn, sounds like we're creating cursed Sisyphus."

"Dr. Hartford, you are Sigmund's greatest supporter. What seems to be the problem?"

"Never mind, return to your spiel."

Fixing her hair, Destiny clears her raspy throat. She wants to punch Chase square in the teeth right now.

"The fourth step is action. The subjects will learn to utilize these new aspects of their being practically. They will behave as we expect them to. No more nonsense. Finally, as these subjects procreate, the subjects will hand their progenies over to us to repeat the process."

"Wait," Chase says, rising to his feet, "this process won't stop?"

"Of course, if we don't instill this into every generation, they may eventually return to their former ignorance."

"So, in a way, the Sigmund project will never end."

"Of course, you already knew this. This was your idea after all," Destiny says, her eyes furrowed. "Any questions or concerns?"

"No. No," Chase stutters, pacing, "it sounds like a perfectly logical process to develop nihilists."

"Dr. Hartford," Destiny raises her voice, "you are overly irritable today. I know you typically have an unlikeable disposition, but this is ridiculous."

"Are you done with your presentation?" Chase asks. Oliver is screaming. His voice is overwhelming. Ringing, Chase's ears feel like they may pop.

"No. I am not. Can you please sit down? We need to discuss what we are going to do with the prototype due to its unique features."

Fidgeting, Chase forces his legs to bend. He can't sit still. He can't. Destiny, hurrying through her slides, wants to leave as soon as possible. Chase seems unpredictable. He keeps grunting, groaning, moving, and twitching. Diagnosing Chase with anxiety inflamed by the developing prototype, Destiny ends her presentation early. He obviously isn't listening to her. He seems to be listening to somebody else. A grating voice in his head.

***

"There are riots in Haspock," Jim, Samantha's cameraman, says. They are sitting in their van, eating lunch. "I got a lead from a source there."

"We can't cover that. Harriet asked us, for the moment, to cover only positive news. We have an appointment with the Orbis Institute Club. They're having a rally and celebration for the upcoming prototype," Samantha replies after biting into her peanut butter and jelly sandwich. She doesn't eat much substance to keep her curvy figure.

"What a bore. People love chaos."

"I know, but Harriet's the boss. If she wants the public to see the world in a particular way, then they're going to see it that way."

"What if, just one time, we reported news that didn't have an agenda? What if we reported chaos that wasn't just propaganda? Or benevolence that wasn't a front for something else?" Jim asks with big eyes. He has always been a dreamer.

Giggling, Samantha playfully slaps Jim's shoulder, "Oh Jim, you're like a wonderstruck child. But we can't do that. It's politics, Jim. Simple politics."

"That's a bummer."

"Well, life is one big bummer. We just got to make the most of it and fuck despair."

Jim's face melts like a blue popsicle. Samantha's right, he thinks to himself.

***

Outside Jarita's apartment, hundreds of people push against a wall of riot police.

"You can't take all of us!" a wiry young man boasts, waving his crimson-stained shirt in the air. Blood trickles down his temple across his bare chest.

"When will we get a return on our investment?" a middle-aged woman cries.

"I want my child! Her name is Sophie! She's only five!" balls a thirty-year-old woman with disheveled black hair.

The police don't respond. They keep corralling the crowd into an inescapable corner pinned between two giant apartment complexes. Weary eyes beat back and forth. Glancing over their shoulders, the mob sees their fate. Growing apprehensive, the lean young man bodyslams the riot shield in front of him. Other rowdy young men do the same, throwing their hardy bodies at the riot police.

Pressing forward, the enforcers don't let up.

"We got to fight! We got to fight!" The wiry young man bellows, pulling a revolver from his pocket. Firing two shots that crack the riot shield, he swears militantly. Shrieks ensue as thunderous bullets rip through the air.

An onslaught of rocks, bricks, and planks rain down on the other side of the wall of shields. Skidding, another SWAT van arrives on the scene. Jumping out the back, armed with grenade launchers, the armored enforcers drop to a knee.

"Fire!" the unit's commander shouts. The launchers roar like dragons as their smokey breath mingles wispily with the air. Yelling in terror, the mob endeavors to flee, but they're trapped. Petrified pests ensnared shoulder to shoulder. Clawing at the riot shield, the wiry young man tries to jump over it.

Exploding brilliantly, like simultaneous fireworks, the grenades decimate the crowd, sending limbs through the air like confetti. Raising his shield after the eruption, a riot policeman sighs. Latching onto his foot, a legless woman with blood gushing from her midsection stares up at him with bulging eyes. Her ghostly face, whitewashed with shock and panic, knocks the air out of him.

Gasping for breath to form the words, she breathes, "I just wanted Sophie. My Sophie." Staring into her desperate eyes, the policeman feels his skin crawl. "I just wanted Sophie." Sucking in a deep breath, he slams the shield down, watching it crush the woman's bug eyes.

***

"Have you looked into their eyes yet?" Oliver asks. He stands before Chase's bed with his olive arms crossed. His eyes pierce through Chase's visage like he's looking into his soul. Shuddering, Chase can't keep his body from shaking. Anxiety, like a tyrannous apparition, won't let him sleep.

"No," Chase replies.

Gazing out the window towards the Orbis Institute, Oliver shakes his head in disappointment. "Is the prototype complete?"

"It's soaking overnight."

"Then what?"

"Then the Psychology Department can have it."

"If this prototype is successful, are you going to create more in the masses?"

"Once the process is efficient enough."

Nodding, Oliver pulls up a wooden chair and sits down with his legs crossed. "How does that make you feel?"

Chase's chattering teeth rack his body. Rubbing the bridge of his nose, Chase clears his throat aggressively. He plays with the blanket at his waist.

"How does that make you feel?" Oliver repeats his question.

"I—I can't get you out of my head. Why won't you get out of my head?"

Smirking, Oliver chuckles. "I was never meant to be out of your head."

"What do you mean?"

"That voice, that conscience of yours, the one you seared so many years ago, especially after the death of your parents. That was me. I was that voice."

"I'm going mental, aren't I?"

"Mental wouldn't be the word I'd use."

"What would you use?"

"Metaphysical, dare I say, spiritual."

"Oh shit. I'm sorry, but I can't be. I'm a scientist, not a mystic."

Laughing, Oliver looks at Chase like a father looks at his developing child, "Whatever gave you the notion that being a scientist meant you are confined to the natural alone?"

"We can't study anything else," Chase replies.

"Ah, that is where your wrong," Oliver says. "You just can't study it the same way you study a rock or a tree. No. One must approach the spiritual as a relationship, not like a science experiment."

"What are you suggesting?"

"I am from beyond the wall," Oliver says as if ignoring Chase's question, "I am not of your world."

"You're in the world, just not Orbis."

"Of course, in the grand scheme of things, I am in this world, but I am by nature much different. My nature is more than physical, as are those subjects you so ruthlessly handle. However, they only know how to pursue nature. I know what truly must be sought after."

"What is that?"

"You must get beyond the wall, to my father's land. There is where freedom lies."

"I can't just run through the wall," Chase protests, sweat oozing from his gaping pores. "How do you expect me to get over that contraption?"

Laughing uneasily, Oliver scratches the back of his head. He pauses for a moment before replying, "I know how it must happen. How I wish it could happen is another story, but I know what must be done."

"What?"

Smiling, Oliver shakes his head, "You're not prepared to hear that part. Not yet."

Chase quakes and shudders. Chills like icy spiders weave webs around his spinal cord. He feels his lungs light on fire. The air seems to be getting thinner. Rising to his feet, Oliver sets his chair over by the prison bars that have appeared. Cold cement closes in around Chase's fainting body. Looking this way and that way, Chase screeches. The ceiling descends. The prison bars grow thicker. His heart pounds like a drum in his ears. Oliver, with a deferential smile, draws by Chase's bedside.

"Chase, look into my eyes."

Chase frantically looks around him. The walls are closing in. He can feel his chest implode.

"Chase, Chase, look into my eyes."

Chase's head grows numb and ripples with anxiety as wrinkles wash over his cheeks.

"Chase, look into my eyes."

Gazing into Oliver's clear eyes, Chase breathes in Oliver's exhale. Touching Chase's forehead with his warm fingers, Oliver whispers, "Awake."

Gasping for air, Chase shoots up in bed. Sweat rolls down the side of his face, soaking the wet bedsheets he rubs between his fingers. Wiping his face and shaking, Chase reaches for his glasses. He takes a breath. He takes several breaths.

Chapter 8

"It was a success!" Destiny marvels, her eyes nearly exploding from their sockets.

"Isn't it brilliant?" Dr. Morey says with a mile-wide smile painted on his face. "Just brilliant."

"When can I have it?" Destiny asks.

"As soon as the downloads are complete."

Chase keeps his head low to hide the bags beneath his eyes, the anchors buried into his flushed cheeks. Looking confused, Dr. Morey throws an arm around Chase.

"My, aren't you a jolly one this morning. Had too much to drink in celebration last night?" he quips. "I know we must be professional, but a cheer would be appropriate. I can overlook just a slight burst of excitement."

Forcing a smile past his whitewashed visage, Chase performs a half-hearted fist pump. Dr. Morey frowns, retracting his arm. Clearing his throat, Dr. Morey turns to Destiny who is grimacing at Chase's melancholy profile.

"Dr. Collins," Dr. Morey says.

"Yes, Dr. Morey."

"I want you to start as soon as possible. When will the download be complete?"

"In a couple hours."

"Perfect. Lead the prototype then to your department and do what you must."

Destiny nods, unable to suppress a smirk. The green lights in the corridor glow eerily across her smooth cheeks. Turning towards Chase, who is kicking a pebble back and forth, Dr. Morey clears his throat.

Looking up from his petty game, Chase says, "Yes, Dr. Morey?"

"I would like you to prepare more subjects."

"More subjects, Dr. Morey? Shouldn't we make sure this prototype cooperates?"

"We don't have time to wait. Besides, I have perfect faith in your abilities. I know you *never* let me down," Dr. Morey says, his eyes intently fixed on Chase's gaze. Chase's insides quiver. "Glad, we had this time together," Dr. Morey says, looking back through the observation window. "So glad." Looking into the Memory Room, Chase watches the prototype's memories burn into its fresh brain. He watches the tube that is displaying the percentage complete get closer to one hundred. Feeling his heart sink, Chase glances at the prototype again. The prototype's eyes are closed.

Thank god. Chase thinks to himself. *Thank god.*

***

After hours, on the verge of nightfall, Chase hangs around outside Animal Enclosure. He slides the door open. Turning the lights on, he walks back towards the rats. The oblivious rats. There's no cruel smile. There's no sign of pleasure. Emptiness resides in Chase's dark eyes. Enticing a rat through the tunnel, Chase shoves its plump body over the edge into the monster's lair. Gobbling it up like a troll, the bobcat purrs. His heart filled with meaty delight.

Frowning, Chase entices another rat. He shoves it over the edge. The bobcat devours it. Watching Chase, it smiles wickedly. Getting another rat, Chase repeats the process. The devilish cat purrs. Cursing under his breath, Chase tempts another rat to its demise. Then another and another. The diabolical cat cackles with delight. Chase's face grows red and burns with indignation. Smoke pours from his scarlet ears.

The last rat, naively rolling in the straw, doesn't know why Chase is watching him so keenly. The hatch opens. Sniffing the air, the stupid rat waddles casually, just craving a morsel of moldy bread. One ugly piece of moldy bread. Dropping another and another, Chase swears uncontrollably like he has an obscene tic. At the edge of destruction, the rat sits on its haunches, chewing on its last meal. Its last blighted meal. Practically stabbing the rat, Chase knocks it off the edge. Glaring, Chase watches the evil cat rear back with a sly gleam in its eye. Pouncing, it crushes the rat between its sharp canines.

"No!" Chase bellows, "No! No! You filthy bastard!" Kicking the bobcat's glass enclosure, Chase yells contentiously. He kicks, swears, and slams his arm against the glass tube of death. Shattering the tube, Chase yells louder. Hissing, the bobcat crouches, occasionally swatting the air. "You think you're scary? Huh? Huh?" Chase antagonizes, kicking the enclosure as hard as he can. Hissing again, the cat crouches lower. Ripping a fire extinguisher off the wall, Chase throws a blanket over the airholes. Chase, drunk on rage, shoves the nozzle into the tube. Hissing louder, the bobcat backs into the farthest corner.

"Take this, you filthy bastard!" Ghost-white, Chase's hand grapples the nozzle like a psychopath. White smoke pouring profusely from the extinguisher clouds the enclosure. Hissing and choking, the cat runs into the glass. It screams and claws. It chokes some more. Not stopping, Chase keeps the extinguisher engaged until nothing but puffs of white residue spit from its exhausted mouth. Throwing the empty can on the floor, Chase waits for the smoke to clear. He covers his mouth and nose. Lying on its side, on top of an off-white pile of dust, the monstrous cat hisses no more.

"Damn you," Chase mutters, "go to hell." Marching out the room, Chase heads for the elevator. It's time to go home and lie awake some more.

Chapter 9

At five in the morning, “Inventions and Sinfonias” playing in the background, Chase prepares the lab for his team. Mumbling, he fumbles with a pair of forceps. Taking five exhausting minutes to set two small forceps down, Chase fidgets with his lab coat. He reaches for a slim flask hidden in his coat pocket. Pulling it out, without a second thought, he downs it all with one swallow. He shoves the empty glass back into his pocket.

“Who are the lucky winners today?” Chase sardonically quips, teetering his head back and forth. Sifting through his stack of notes, he stops at a list of fifteen subjects. “Subject 240, 469, 591, 34, 780, 11, 999, 223, 876, 75, 611, 300, 804, 172, and 1250.” Chase squints, “Wait, he wants to dig into the reserves?” Sweating, Chase trembles. His palpitating heart threatens to break through his chest. “The reserves?” He turns around. Revolving on his heels, he looks at each freezer with horror. He envisions thousands upon thousands of freezers.

“Impossible,” Chase whispers.

“Dr. Hartford,” Dr. Morey calls, stepping into the lab. He wears a proper suit, black tie, and polished shoes. Drawn across his chest, his pocket watch shimmers.

“Dr. Morey,” Chase croaks.

“I see you are setting up for today,” Dr. Morey comments, straightening the forceps Chase set in place.

“Yes, of course.”

“Will we be able to get through the fifteen subjects planned for today?”

"Yes, fif—fifteen," Chase stutters, glancing down at his notes.

Eyeing Chase, Dr. Morey asks, "Does there seem to be a problem? You look paler than usual."

"You want us to dig into the reserves?"

"Of course, every subject will eventually need to go through the process. I chose subjects that are very different from each other to see the results. You dictated those numbers yesterday. Don't you recall?"

"It must have slipped my mind that we were digging in the reserves."

"Not to worry, I already had that subject dismembered ahead of time. You just have to bring the cart over to the lab."

"Good. Good," Chase mutters, scratching his face.

Frowning, Dr. Morey squeezes Chase's shoulder, "Dr. Hartford, I know there has been a lot of stress lately with the Sigmund Project approaching its climax, but I assure you it'll be fine. Samantha is covering pleasant news, the public, in general, is at peace with our progress despite the riot, and we s—"

"Riot?" Chase asks, his eyes wide.

"Yes, I thought you heard about it."

"No, I didn't. What was it about?"

"No need to trouble yourself with the details."

"What was it about?" Chase asks again, grappling the end of the table.

Sighing, Dr. Morey says, "An impoverished woman refused to support the Sigmund Project and tried to keep a subject. Once word got around, some of the people in the area started a small tumult. Nothing too serious."

"Dear god," Chase mutters, "why is this happening?"

Squeezing his shoulder harder this time, Dr. Morey grabs Chase's attention. "Dr. Hartford, do not bother with the public. Focus on the task at hand. We are on the verge of a breakthrough. You are revolutionizing the future."

Nodding, Chase fiddles with his lab coat. Taking a deep breath, Dr. Morey tugs at his pocket watch nervously, "Dr. Hartford, I also wanted to notify you that I will need you to share your research with the other teams at Orbis Institute."

"Why?" Chase asks, looking up from his coat pocket.

"I want Sigmund to be in full motion as soon as possible. It will take far too long to have one team handling all the subjects. I gave every team the go-ahead to abandon their current projects so they can focus on Sigmund."

"How many subjects would we be able to get through in a day then?"

"Hundreds if not thousands," Dr. Morey replies with a devilish grin.

"Dear god."

"I know it is astronomical. The future is in our grasps. Soon Orbis will be free from its self-destructive behaviors. It will be free. Free, I say."

Chase doesn't reply; he stares into an unseen void. His bottom lip quivers.

"Will you share your research with the other team leaders?" Dr. Morey asks, staring into Chase's hollow eyes.

"Ye—yes, Dr. Morey," Chase stutters.

"Good. Very good."

"Dear god, oh dear god."

Dawdling through the eldritch glow, Chase takes small steps through the underground corridors. The green lights whir, making the floor look like a harrowing swamp. Turning into the Dismemberment hallway, Chase freezes. His eyes stare at the water-tight, stainless steel, door at the end of the corridor. Subject Reserve.

Chase remembers the mad rush that fateful day. Vans and trucks packed with subjects rolled into Orbis Institute's garage. Shuffling the subjects along, beating the rebellious in place, enforcers loaded them into the elevator. Shackled, gagged, and locked together, the subjects marched in line through that foreboding door. Thousands and thousands of subjects, like chain-gangs, were led to their prison cells. Only elect Orbis Institute members, Chase being one of them, were allowed in the corridors to organize the chaos.

He remembers assigning the subjects their cells. He remembers pointing his stylus at the door numbers, calling out the subject numbers like he was herding cattle. Crossing off the numbers from his tablet, he went down the aisles, segregating the subjects based on particular features — color, size, age, and sex. He was efficient. Very efficient.

"Dear god," Chase mutters, "oh, Oliver, forgive me." Swallowing his emotions, Chase presses forward. Swiping his card, Dismemberment opens. Neatly organized by the door is subject 1250's cart. White shrouds that smell of disinfectant blanket the cart's three racks. Pulling latex gloves from a flimsy box, Chase grabs the crisp handle. The room is a giant freezer box. Trying his best to ignore the metal contraption in the center of the room, Chase closes his left eye. He can't stand to look at the horrendous machine. Those who know about it dubbed it the "Grim Reaper."

"Dear god," Chase whispers, leaving Dismemberment.

***

Chase wails passionately. Other prisoners crane their necks through their barred windows to get a look. On his knees, Chase feels like he just got railed by a freight train. Immediately after the guard left, he broke down. Oliver, sitting next to him with his eyes closed and head against the wall, prays. His lips form silent words. Puddling, Chase's tears soak through his pants. Burnt with anguish, his face is bright red. Oliver sets an arm around Chase. He sniffles, wipes his nose and dabs a lingering tear. Sitting up, he looks over at Oliver.

"I sent my research to the other teams," he says in between sharp breaths.

"Take your time," Oliver whispers gently, "take a couple of deep breaths. Close your eyes and settle." Closing his eyes, Chase meditates for a second. He gathers his thoughts together. He feels his chest loosen, and the lump in his throat dissolves. Opening his eyes, Oliver looks over at Chase. "Now," he says, "what did you want to say?"

"I sent my research to other teams," Chase repeats, his voice clear, "We have gone through thousands of subjects already."

"Do you know how long it will be until you're complete?"

"Once everything gets fine-tuned. I wouldn't be surprised to see the Subject Reserve be emptied in a couple weeks. Orbis Institute has poured all its time, money, resources, and energy into this project. It is going to be complete as soon as possible," Chase says, his words beginning to slur together by the end.

"Calm down," Oliver says, "calm down. I realize it's only a matter of time."

"How do you know?"

Grinning, Oliver replies, "I know things, but I also know it won't succeed."

"How are you so sure?"

"Because I'm here."

"You're in prison."

"I'm where I need to be."

Frowning, Chase's head dips. He says, "I wish I had that kind of faith."

"You will."

"I can't stop," Chase whispers. "I'm afraid. Terribly afraid."

"What are you afraid of?"

"I'll lose everything if I try to stop this madness," Chase says, his voice rising. "I'll lose my house, my job, my reputation, my life, even. I'll get killed."

"Oh, no. It'll be worse than that," Oliver says, his face stern.

"What?"

"You'll be kicked out of Orbis all together. You'll be evicted from this place with the whole city's back turned on you."

"Oh, no," Chase groans, tucking his head between his knees, "Oh, god, there has to be another way."

Laying his hand on Chase's back, Oliver says, "No, I'm afraid not, but there is hope."

"What hope?" Chase asks, looking over at Oliver.

"My father's land, yes, it lies beyond these walls. He is much better than anything Orbis has to offer."

"Your father or his land?"

"Both, but the land is only blessed because he is the inherently blessed."

"How far is it from the walls?"

"It is, I must say, a journey. Some would describe it as a trek through hell itself, but it is there."

"How can I trust you?" Chase asks, his voice cracking. He feels like he may cry again. Resting a tender hand on Chase's bony shoulder, Oliver gazes into his eyes. For a moment, Chase feels a rush of peace sweep over him. No more words are needed.

Leaving the prison, a twenty-minute drive from his place, Chase sits behind the wheel of his coupe. Sighing, he plops his head against the headrest. He feels, to a certain degree, peaceful, but he isn't ready. Not yet. He doesn't make rash decisions, not decisions this big. Starting his car, he checks his fuel. Ten gallons remain of bio-fuel, an ingenious fuel source created by Orbis Institute, derived from algae. Since oil was no longer available, Orbis Institute had to develop a solution after the panic.

Cruising through Lockhaven, on the other side of Paddington, Chase whistles to himself. This is the first time in a long time that he feels assured. He may actually fall asleep tonight. Making his way through a dark street shadowed by a vast, industrial factory, Chase stops at a flickering red light. The traffic light, on its last leg, dangles from a fraying chord. Blinking slowly, like a heart monitor going flat, it holds Chase in place. The streets are empty.

"Crap," Chase mutters, growing impatient. About ready to run the light, Chase's foot hovers over the pedal.

"Aaaah!" Gunshots rumble, ripping through the air. Glancing over his shoulder, Chase sees a pair of shadowy figures by the factory's cooling unit. One large figure towers over a limp figure dangling on his arm. The large one, by what Chase can tell, looks almost like an enforcer. Turning, the foreboding figure sees Chase hasn't moved. The light is green.

"Shit!" Chase yells, jolting forward. A couple of shots buzz by his window like wasps. "Shit!"

***

"So, you're not just here for a social call?" Samantha asks, leaning on her chaise lounge. She wears a ruby slit dress. Her left leg, a tanned beauty, lays across the cushion. Reclining in a fluffy, white chair, Rob smirks.

"Not exactly," he says. His voice is rough, but in an attractive, bad-boy kind of way, "Harriet wanted me to drop by before I went home."

"I assume for good reason."

"Of course." Standing, Rob walks over to a wine chiller, a rare commodity. Choosing a merlot, he rests it on the kitchen table. Looking over at Samantha, he raises a glass and asks, "Do you mind?"

"Pour me a glass as well," she replies, waving her hand. Her glittery nails sparkle beneath the chandelier. Pouring two glasses of wine, Rob gives one to Samantha and sits back down on his chair. He's a ruddy guy with curly red hair and fair skin. Compared to his older sister, Harriet, Rob is a model. He definitely received the better genes.

"What did your big sis want?" Samantha asks, taking a sip from her glass.

Swirling his glass, Rob stares at the chandelier, "She had a lead."

"She could have messaged me for that."

"Well, this one is... complicated," Rob says, taking his first sip.

"Of course it is. Everything is complicated these days."

Snorting, Rob takes another sip. He says, "According to a witness, there has been a shooting in Lockhaven."

Picking up her tablet from the coffee table, Samantha types notes. Her glass of wine sits in the tablet's place.

"Any more details?"

"Of course," Rob says, taking another sip. "Aren't you privileged?"

Confused by the change of topic, Samantha furrows her eyebrows, "What do you mean?"

"I mean, you're the only goddamn news station this city has. You're the only channel for that manner. Even though I wish we could bring TV back again," shaking his head, he takes another sip, "you get all the fun. All the stories."

"Rob, what is the rest of the story at hand?" Samantha asks, frowning.

"Oh, yes," he laughs, downing the rest of his glass, "a protestor, presumably associated with Oliver, murdered an innocent Sigmund Project supporter."

"I'm allowed to cover chaos again?"

"Of course, as long as it's chaos that propels us forward."

"Sure," Samantha mumbles, finishing her notes. "Anything else?"

"Make it known that the Orbis Institute is responding to the incident with charity. They're donating a chunk of change to the Orbis Institute Club and the victim's family, just as she would have wanted it."

"Oh, how generous," Samantha says sarcastically. She pushes a strand of hair behind her ear. Finishing her notes, Samantha sets her tablet down. Practically chugging the rest of her drink, she sinks farther into her chaise lounge. Rob walks over to Samantha, a wad of cash in his left hand.

"Here," Rob says, handing the money over to Samantha, "Harriet wanted you to have it."

Sitting up, Samantha takes the money eagerly. Flipping through the hundreds, she whispers, "Two grand and couple on top. Not bad."

"I slipped in the extra hundreds," Rob says, smiling. His pearly teeth glisten. Sighing, unable to hide a grin, Samantha stands. Her left thigh gently presses against Rob's torso. She leans towards his ear with her velvet lips.

"I supposed that generous tip had an alternative motive," she whispers seductively.

"I mustn't have been the first," he replies.

"Certainly not."

"Well, where do you want to begin?"

"You lead." Grabbing the zipper on the back of Samantha's dress, Rob smiles devilishly as he undressed her. Samantha giggles, "That's where they all start."

***

"She was my sister's boyfriend's brother's wife, and she attended the stupid Orbis Institute Club once," Jim grumbles, ripping a bite out of his sandwich.

"What are you saying, Jim?" Samantha asks. She finished her lunch a couple of minutes ago. Jim is only halfway through his. He's been spending most of his lunch break ranting.

"All I'm saying is that I knew her."

"How well?"

"We hung out a couple of times, nothing serious, but still. I knew her."

"Come on, Jim. What are you suggesting? That there's some big conspiracy?"

Slamming his hand into the steering wheel, Jim curses as he realizes his sandwich was in that hand. Lettuce and tomatoes slathered in mayonnaise plop onto the floor. "Shit," he mutters, throwing the rest of his sandwich out the window.

"Calm down, Jim," Samantha says, seemingly indifferent. Crossing her arms, she sits back in her seat.

"Calm down? I don't think you understand. There *is* something going on. Ever since Orbis announced that damn prototype, everyone is in some sort of trance. Those who aren't a part of that trance get shot or blown sky-high."

"Maybe the majority is right to trust the institute and everyone else is crazy."

"Oh, screw off," Jim growls, "I swear something is up, but all we do is support damn politics that don't give a shit about people, only agendas. We should have covered that riot. We should dig into this murder. I swear to you, the last thing Jenny would have wanted is for the institute to throw money at her club and family. Not like she has much say now being dead and all."

"Get over it, Jim," Samantha snaps, "it's a tragedy. I'm sorry, but get over it. Sure, it's politics. Sure, it's a shit show, but fuck despair. Play the game and win. Stop trying to be some kind of camera toting hero. What are you going to do besides make everything worse and get yourself killed or ostracized? Forget it."

"Look, I'm tired of being a gear in the system! You might like being a political whore, but I don't! Jenny got murdered and not as some sort of Orbis Institute guru, but as an actual normal human who knows the institute doesn't give a shit about us. Not like she or anyone can—"

"Shut up!"

"No!" Jim hollers, his veins bulging from his neck, "I'm not done! Why aren't we allowed inside? Why did they have to take every single kid and tell us it'll be ok? And people bought it! People bought it! Those who don't buy it wind up pulverized!"

"How many degrees do you have, Jim?" Samantha retorts, her nails clawing at her seat, "Huh? I don't have any. Neither do you. They know what's best."

"I don't need a degree to prove I have a head! I regularly read, if you were curious. I just know shit when I smell it."

"Well, you didn't seem to really care until it affected you. What does that say?"

"It says I was foolish."

"Oh yeah? What are you going to do now since you're so enlightened?"

Jim goes quiet. Samantha snorts, sitting back in her chair.

"That's what I thought," she huffs. "Orbis Institute is in the center of the city. It is our heart. Attack it, and you kill yourself."

"I hate Orbis."

"You know what," Samantha mutters, "just fuck it and smile."

Chapter 10

Sitting on his recliner, Chase drinks a cold beer. He watches a report shot earlier in the day regarding yesterday's murder. Closing his eyes, Chase can still hear the shriek. He can see the towering figure holding the corpse in his arm. Chase never told anyone. Who was he going to tell? The killer was most likely an enforcer who had a mission given to him by someone up top. Sighing, Chase opens his eyes. It doesn't help his conscience that he got to watch another several hundred subjects get passed off to the Psychology Department.

"The killer, yet to be identified, is suspected to be a Sigmund protestor," Samantha reports, standing outside the industrial factory where the murder took place. "Inspired by Oliver, the killer is thought to have murdered Jenny Miller because she was a devout Orbis Institute Club member."

Frowning, Chase sits up. Although he didn't get a clear view, he is reasonably certain it wasn't a protestor who murdered Jenny. He didn't look like that type. Besides Orbis Institute Club members aren't the targets of protestors. Many club members aren't particularly wealthy or influential, they simply are people who hope to gain something from the institute. The club doesn't hold any sort of voting or legislative power that affects how the institute operates. The club is basically a public relations team that speaks positively about the institute and demonstrates their support publicly via word of mouth or advertising, obtaining small rewards for their dedication.

If a protestor would go out of their way to murder one of those members, it would be a waste of their time unless they targeted a wealthy donor.

Expounding upon the available details, which aren't many, Samantha finishes her report by notifying the public that the Orbis Institute is giving a hefty lump sum to the Orbis Institute Club and Jenny's family.

"That," Chase snorts, "is a joke." Turning off the tube, Chase heads upstairs for his bed. He had enough of Samantha for one night.

***

"He's just sitting there," Titus whispers to Greta. In the corner of the room, Chase stares into space. He doesn't appear to be mad, nor does he seem happy. A melancholy disposition has settled over him. Uneasy, the scientists in the lab whisper among themselves. Whirring, the lights flicker. "I hope the power doesn't go out again," Titus mutters, lifting a bone from a basin. Soaked in a crimson fluid, the humerus thickens. The liquid seeps into the cracks and crevices, strengthening the bone.

"Isn't it crazy?" Greta says, "Isn't it crazy how we're able to make—"

"Stop," Titus whispers harshly.

"What?"

Looking around at the freezers, Titus replies, "I don't want to think about it."

"You work here."

"Doesn't mean I like to think about it. It still gives me chills."

Shrugging, Greta cleans an ulna, "I think it's encouraging to know we're advancing Orbis. You got to look at it like that."

"I try."

"Trust me. Once this is over, we'll reap the benefits."

"Sure."

"Dr. Hartford," a tall, lanky scientist calls.

"What do you want, Dr. Larky?" Chase asks after an exasperated sigh.

"I believe we may be missing a couple of organs for subject 15,421."

"You want me to check?" Chase asks dryly.

"Yes, if you could."

"What organs would I be looking for?"

"Pancreas and the liver."

"Ok."

Taking his time, Chase heads for the elevator. A pair of scientists discussing data gives Chase side-eyes. Neither of them has ever been allowed in that elevator. Curiosity piques their attention. Ignoring them, Chase enters the metal box and selects the basement. He watches the door slide shut. The cab lurches.

Flashbacks, like vexing dreams, sprint through his head. A sinewy subject with bulging eyes and thin lips squirmed out of Chase's grip. Haring through the sinister corridors, it found an emergency exit — a giant steel door with a massive red rod bolted across its face. Unable to reach the handle to yank the rod back into its shaft and out of the box, the subject looked over its shoulder in terror. Approaching it with a cold stare, Chase closed in on the rat. Scraping at the door with its little nails, it squeaked out of despair. It wanted moldy bread. The enforcers told the subject that it would be safe, that the institute would defend it. At that moment, scratching at the steel door with a prowling bobcat preparing to pounce, the rat knew better. It knew the moldy bread was only a mirage. Squealing for mercy, it curled into a ball, its pink toes near its pointy nose. Snarling, its dark eyes set on its prey, the diabolic cat scoured the rat with its claws. It tore into the small ball of flesh and devoured what was left inside the enclosure. The monster, the baleful cat, left behind a pile of bones. A carcass that germs roving Orbis Institute finished off.

Lurching to a stop, the cab breaks Chase free from his daze. Proceeding through the halls of damnation, Chase keeps his head low. Shame, an anchor weighing on his heart, pulls him down. He slouches over like a drunken stupor. Wearying his mind, memories toy with him like Beelzebub's offspring.

"God, I can't do this," Chase mutters, cupping his ears. He rubs his throbbing temples. Passing by Animal Enclosure, keeping his eyes fixed on the floor, Chase opens Dismemberment. Like a cacodemon wrenched his head towards the Grim Reaper, Chase stares into its translucent eyes.

Foreboding, its girth consumes center stage. Shaped like a person bolted together by Satan, it boasts harrowing needles at its hands. Cuffs for wrists, it flexes steel arms laced with saws capable of performing the most precise cuts. Built like a tank for Satan's army of fallen angels, it wears a sable breastplate capable of harvesting organs like potatoes. The legs, the horrid legs, like metallic centipedes, can bend in any direction. They, too, have blades wherever a cut is needed. Needles skewer the monster's boots. Chase's eyes meet the Grim Reaper's eyes as he groans. He stares into the ghastly things. A helmet, better fit for a reprobate, designed to suffocate its victims, sits on the Grim Reaper's head. Two cloudy, grey eyepieces are lodged in the helmet so if the killer desires to watch its victim's soul slip away, he or she can do so with twisted delight. Moaning, Chase remembers. He remembers being one of those killers, but their eyes are vague. He doesn't remember them. Not vividly. He mustn't have cared to notice. He mustn't have known what he was doing.

"Oh, God of Oliver," Chase whispers, "oh, help me." Shaking the blood back into his fingers, he breaks his feet free from cold dread. Reluctantly, he opens the freezer, searching for the number 15,421. A small bin buried in the back of the massive freezer behind freshly dismembered subjects is labeled 15,421. Pushing the larger containers aside, Chase grabs the small bin checking it apprehensively. It's what he needed to get. Closing the freezer door, he hurries out into the corridor.

"Dr. Hartford!" Dr. Morey calls. By his side is Dr. Afreet, the most experienced Grim Reaper operator.

"Hello, Dr. Morey," Chase says flatly.

"Dr. Afreet, please, go ahead and get to your work," Dr. Morey says, pointing at Dismemberment.

"Of course, Dr. Morey," Dr. Afreet says, hardly acknowledging Chase. Still holding onto the small bin, Chase looks at Dr. Morey emptily. All the respect he used to have for Dr. Morey has vanished. All that remains is disgust, bitter disgust.

"Do you need me, Dr. Morey?" Chase asks, hoping the answer is a no.

"I was told I could find you down here."

"Here I am. What do you need?"

"I got word that you have been dropping by the Lockhaven prison rather consistently," Dr. Morey says matter-of-factly. He doesn't look particularly angry, only mildly irritated.

Clearing his throat, Chase fidgets with the bin in hand, "I—who told you that?"

"Doesn't matter," Dr. Morey says curtly. "You also seem to have some sort of unhealthy obsession with Oliver's cell."

"I would hardly call it an obsession."

"That doesn't really matter. An addict normally doesn't know they're an addict."

Hot blood rushes Chase's face. He indignantly retorts, "I wanted to study his claims. Prove them to be false."

"Like a real scientist?"

"Yes, like a real scientist."

"Well, what's your conclusion?"

Pausing, Chase stutters for a moment before blubbering, "He's a fool."

Raising a thick eyebrow, Dr. Morey lets out a rolling sigh. His 270-pound body rumbles. Scratching his temple, he replies, "That didn't sound very convincing."

Growing red, Chase says, "Are you suggesting that I'm some kind of fanatic or mystic?"

"Of course not, Dr. Hartford. Once a man of science, always a man of science."

"Well, good."

"But," Dr. Morey says, raising a thick index finger, "a man of science could have a change in goals. Could, through persuasion, be derailed from his original purpose."

"Dr. Morey—"

"I'm not, by any means, accusing you of such treason. I am, with good reason, concerned for your mental health."

"Dr. Morey—"

"You have been far from being yourself. You are sullen, ill-mannered, and don't think for a second I thought anyone other than you ravaged the Animal Enclosure. It was an absolute travesty before I had to send a subject in there to clean the mess."

"A subject?"

"It was the next on the list. Does that matter? The point is if I get wind that you are visiting that Oliver character again, I will have no other choice but use force to keep you from visiting that criminal."

Grumbling inaudibly, Chase grits his teeth.

"Do we have an understanding, Dr. Hartford?" Dr. Morey asks, his hands strategically placed behind his back.

"Yes, Dr. Morey," Chase sneers.

"Good. Very good."

Later that day, after work, Chase drives for Lockhaven Prison. Dr. Morey's stern face, laced with gloating power, warns Chase to cease this behavior. He can't. Imagining Dr. Morey wielding a scepter, Chase can envision his execution. Chills run down his back. He can't dwell on those thoughts. Not right now.

Arriving at the prison, Chase passes through the security gate with two pairs of eyes burning through his head. He can feel the snipers on the wall watching him. Every guard knows. They all know. Today will be his last visit, his final free pass into Oliver's world. Eyeing Chase with a condemning stare, the secretary, a stone-faced officer, directs him through the security check. Nodding their heads at each other, the guards acknowledge that Chase has nothing on him.

"Dr. Hartford," the taller guard says, hiding behind a pair of reflective sunglasses. Turning around, Chase nods his head, acknowledging the officer. "Dr. Morey told me if you showed up again that you ain't coming back again. Make this one count."

"Thanks for the heads up," Chase says, turning back around.

"So, this is you're last visit?" Oliver asks as soon as the cell door closes.

"I'm afraid so," Chase mutters, still standing. Oliver, standing as well, approaches Chase confidently.

Lowering his head near Chase's ear, he whispers, "Make this one count."

"That's what he—"

"Shh," Oliver hushes Chase, his eyes looking out through his window, "I know. I know."

Looking over his shoulder uneasily, Chase fixes his glasses.

"What is the plan exactly?" Chase asks, "I'm not ready to commit to anything."

Grabbing Chase's shoulder, Oliver gazes deep into his dark eyes, "You will soon. Sigmund is soon complete, is it not?"

"Yes."

"The last subject will be yours. Dr. Morey is going to give you the honor."

"The honor?" Chase asks, his tongue tasting sour.

"It's not an honor, but that's how he will see it. Then, when you look into her eyes, you will understand."

A shudder courses through Chase's body. "Her?"

"Yes. I want you to, afterward, go and see the rest. Observe them. Listen. Watch."

"You mean the other subjects?"

"Yes. Examine the Psychology Department. You are aware they store your *subjects* in their cells overnight? Right?"

"Of course. How do you know that?" Chase asks, his heart racing.

"I'm from beyond the wall. I can see clearly."

"Even what you can—"

"Not right now," Oliver interrupts, "I can explain another time. Right now, I just need to explain what is necessary. We don't have much time."

"Where was this weeks ago?" Chase protests, a feeling of frustration swelling in his chest.

"You weren't ready then. Wisdom, compassion, empathy were foreign words weeks ago. But now, right now, you are beginning to see."

Chase stutters gibberish. He can't seem to get his thoughts straight.

"Hush now," Oliver rebukes, passion burning inside his bright eyes, "hush. Please, sit and listen."

Chase sits on the edge of the bed obediently.

"My father, Christian, told me it's my time. I—"

"Explain—"

"Hush now," Oliver hisses, "We will have an eternity to discuss the details, but right now, just listen."

An eternity. Chase thinks to himself. *What does he mean?*

Sensing his worry, Oliver slows down, "Chase, time works differently beyond the wall. I know you don't understand now, but you will. Trust me."

Chase feels a wave of peace wash over him. His nerves calm.

"Ok," he replies.

"As I was saying," Oliver continues, "my father notified me that my time has come. It's my time to save Orbis from its inevitable destruction. This coming week, you must visit me after you look into the final subject's eyes. You must, at the dead of night, come to my cell."

"At the dead of night?"

"Yes, it must be at night. Do not fear. I will be with you."

"With me? You're here."

"Yes, in the flesh, I am here, but my presence goes beyond my flesh. I will be with you. You must trust me." Oliver's gaze, a refreshing pool, washes over Chase's anxious nerves once again. "We will gather the subjects and make a dash for the wall."

"There are over 20,000 subjects in the reserve!" Chase exclaims, growing red after realizing how loud he shouted. Lowering his voice, he repeats, "Over 20,000."

"I know," Oliver replies, "They're going to be our army."

"They're so young. How are they an army?"

"Oh, you have never seen childlike faith at its best," Oliver says, a whimsical smile filling his cheeks. "I dare say it is one of the most powerful weapons this world has."

"What about their parents?" Chase asks, struggling to keep his voice low. The excitement in the air is thick.

Oliver's face sinks. "They're time will come, but not then. I'm afraid they must suffer a little longer."

"Why?"

"You'll understand later," Oliver says, his voice choked with tears. "These children must first drink from my father's oasis. You must, too," he adds with a warm smile.

"I must drink? Or I will want to drink?"

"Both."

Chase scratches his face. He doesn't know what he's getting himself into.

"What are we going to do once we're running? Where are we going to take all those subjects if we can even keep them together?" Chase asks. The whole ordeal seems so daunting. It appears impossible.

"We'll be running after the wall, after the only gate the frightful barrier has."

"Whoever tries that is going to get themselves killed," Chase blubbers, growing pale. "It's a steel curtain. It's impossible."

"I'll split that curtain," Oliver says, that passionate flame burning behind his eyes like a bonfire.

"How?"

"That's my job," Oliver says, his face sinking again.

"What are you going to do?"

"You'll see," Oliver whispers. Smiling warmly, he laughs, "It'll be worth it, Chase. It'll all be worth it. Trust me."

"Supposing this all works, what am I going to do? I don't know anything about what's beyond."

"It'll become clear with time," Oliver assures him. "Trust my voice."

"I don't understand," Chase whispers. Filling with courage, a new pair of eyes seems to lighten his previously dark eyes. "But," Chase says, with a booming voice, "I will."

"You will."

Pablo escorts Chase from the cell. Leading him by the arm, Pablo has his eyes set on the exit.

"I'll take him from here on out," the tall guard from earlier says. Pablo doesn't protest as he leaves Chase to the tall guard with reflective shades. Taking Chase through a nearby door labeled Peter's Office, the tall guard offers Chase a seat. Checking the windows, the tall guard closes the blinds and locks the door.

"My name's Peter," the tall guard says. "I have orders from Dr. Morey to get you to sign this." Peter tosses a small manilla envelope on the small coffee table to the left of Chase. Taking a seat at his desk, Peter clasps his hands together. "Dr. Hartford, I'm afraid you'll no longer be able to come here until further notice. Sorry, it's simply orders."

Opening the envelope, Chase finds a packet of papers.

"What is this all about?" Chase asks, flipping through the packet.

"Dr. Morey just wants you to sign those papers there acknowledging that you consent to this peculiar restraining order."

"That doesn't sound like something Dr. Morey would do."

Grinning, Peter removes his glasses. A pair of emerald eyes look at Chase.

"Well, I don't make the rules, Dr. Hartford. However, you certainly have the right to take those home and hand them directly to Dr. Morey. I'm sure that would be sufficient."

Furrowing his eyebrows, Chase inspects the documents more closely. Somebody wrote them in a different language. He doesn't know all the words, but some are written in Latin.

"Paperwork is Latin to me," Peter remarks. "I hardly understand it. I'm sure you'll be able to sort through it and read the fine print."

"I haven't studied Latin since my scholastic years."

"Certainly, a scholar as yourself would have a dictionary. Besides, it's all a figure of speech. If you have any questions, Dr. Morey should most certainly be able to answer them."

Drying, Chase's mouth feels like a dessert. Walking over to his side, Peter opens the blinds, unlocks the door, and looks down at Chase. He smiles diplomatically. He says, "Have a good week. Make it count."

"Thanks. You too," Chase croaks.

***

"Thanks for seeing me," Harriet says, her freckled face twisted in worry.

"Have a seat, Harriet," Dr. Morey says, pointing at the leather chair before his desk. Sitting, Harriet mumbles to herself. The chair groans as if to be praying for her to leave.

"Dr. Morey," Harriet says, obviously flustered, "I got another report that Dr. Hartford has visited Oliver."

Grinding his teeth, Dr. Morey leans back in his chair. Fiddling with his pocket watch, he glances out the window. He grabs his touchpad. Typing a note, Dr. Morey swears under his breath.

"I heard he wept inside the cell one time," Harriet blubbers. "He has whispered to and even seems to be friends with Oliver. He is persistent. He—"

"I understand, Harriet!" Dr. Morey roars. Although he never disliked Harriet, Dr. Morey always hated her tendency to exasperate over stressful situations. She doesn't shut up. At least she is good at what she does.

"Sorry, Dr. Morey."

"It's fine. It'll be fine. Just follow the procedure we discussed. If Dr. Hartford tries to revisit the damn prison, meet him with great force. If that doesn't work, I'll handle the rest."

"Yes, Dr. Morey. Of course."

"Well," Dr. Morey grumbles, "get to it." Hurrying for her office, Harriet scuttles away like a dog with her tail between her legs.

***

Chase sits up in bed with his Latin dictionary to his left. The slim packet, lit by a lamp, is flipped open to the last page. A paper with notes scribbled over it is on his right. Translating the packet, Chase discovers that most of the paragraphs are nonsensical lettering, just random letters grouped together. However, every other sentence has at least one real Latin word. Typically, the term is the first word in the sentence. Numbers spotted across the pages are at the end of sentences with Latin words to indicate that the number is useful.

Writing down the last word, Chase removes his glasses. Rubbing his eyes, he sits back against the wall. He can hardly take it all in. This is real. Feeling the bed for the piece of paper, Chase nudges it with his index finger. Picking it up, he takes a deep breath.

The night after the last subject is complete, message Peter the word FREEDOM. His touch pad number is 877-902. He will pick you up in his truck. Sneaking you through the prison, he will release Oliver. The two of you will free the subjects. Take the emergency exit. Head for the main road that divides Paddington and Boltstock. Oliver will open the gate and run towards the oasis.

"That's the plan?" Chase asks himself; his echo falls void on his ears. It doesn't seem real. "That's the grand plan?" He shudders with fear. Yet, unbeknownst to him, a little fire, like the one Oliver has, settled behind his eyes. His courage has come to life.

Chapter 11

Greta and Titus sit at a square table eating lunch together. Orbis Institute's cafeteria is a very simplistic gray cube. Churning, whirring, and whining plays faintly in the background as the machines in the kitchen stir the bland soup, mix repulsive slop packed full of vitamins, and throw together average salads. Friendly banter permeates the room. Growing light-hearted with Sigmund soon completed, many of the Orbis Institute employees have started to loosen up. Those in the government sector look forward to a reposeful Orbis. The scientists, anxiously awaiting less stressful workdays, discuss what they plan to do with their free time. Some even propose fanciful vacations, weeks away from work. Jocular, they laugh about all the good times they will have. The educators, who occupy only a couple floors, chat about the expected adjustments to their current curriculum. Of course, other small colleges spotted across Orbis are currently reviewing their syllabi and are awaiting further direction from Orbis Institute on what is necessary to best suit the Sigmund Project results. Expected change is finally being fleshed out.

Poking his food, Titus has hardly eaten any of his salad. The leaves, wilting around their taupe edges, are not appealing. Neither are the less than ripe tomato slices layered on top, but Titus usually doesn't have a problem finishing his meals. Feeling somewhat effervescent, Greta talks as she finishes her lunch. Gulping water from her glass, she shakes her head, "Sigmund is soon complete." Excitement electrifies her tone of voice. Titus weakly continues to probe a tomato slice as she asks, "Aren't you excited?"

Titus shrugs, "I guess."

"We're advancing. We're moving forward," Greta gushes, her face beaming, "and what's best of all is that we will reap the benefits. All of us will see a better future. We will fix the delusional brain of evolved dreamers. Orbis is all there is, and the new subjects will be torn down to be built back up new again! The correction of evolution!" Trembling with bottled delirium, Greta smiles. Her thin body shivers. Her smile widens farther.

"I just don't know if it was worth it, or if we couldn't have thought of a better way."

"Titus," Greta says, her voice tender, "it doesn't look pleasant, but that is only because Dr. Hartford made it that way. If we didn't have an asshole as our leader, I'm sure even you would be excited, like me." She sighs. "I hate working under him, but what keeps me going is seeing the future. Remember, Titus, that the betterment of Orbis awaits us. We *will* reap the benefits."

Burying his doubts, Titus smiles. He says, "I'm sure you're right. I just feel unreasonably uneasy."

Laying her hand gently on Titus's twitching fingers, Greta's soft eyes rest on his distressed countenance. Her eyes, momentarily, give Titus a sense of tranquility. Intertwining her fingers with his, Greta whispers sweetly, "It'll be ok."

Nodding his head, Titus replies, "I believe you."

***

"Despite your errant behavior by visiting Oliver after my rebuke," Dr. Morey booms, pacing behind his desk, "I will still grant you the honor of handling the last subject."

"Thank you, Dr. Morey," Chase mumbles, the words tasting like wormwood. Marching over by his window, Dr. Morey summons Chase. Reluctantly, Chase joins him.

"Tell me, what do you see?" Dr. Morey asks. His voice is level and threatening, as if there is a correct answer. Clearing his throat, Chase looks over the city. People scurry like mice across the dirty streets. They scamper to and fro, in and out of unsound buildings. Many have given up; they don't want to work. Many hope for a better world and trust Orbis Institute to provide that. Some, the wishful few, pray something lies beyond that wall, something that makes their lives worth the effort. Chase sees the streets. He sees the people, the despair, the rotting buildings, the broken dreams, but behind it all, he sees the wall, the towering wall. Mocking their distress, it has created a daunting façade, a barricade to reality.

Wetting his lips, Chase says, "I see the wall. I see people trapped inside a wall like rats."

Gritting his teeth, Dr. Morey, his voice still level, replies, "I see safety. I see what matters. I see a deteriorating Orbis, people constantly searching for a purpose and being crushed when they find their purpose thwarted. I see Sigmund as a solution. I see," Dr. Morey thunders, his voice getting louder, "people united for a purpose. One goddamn purpose that they can all strive for and stop asking for more. Grind those stupid aspirations to dust and make them drink from Orbis's cauldron and get drunk with *my* purpose. They can go fuck despair and get on with their meaningless lives!" Snapping his head around, boiling with rage, Dr. Morey lunges at Chase. Usurping both his shoulders, Dr. Morey, his eyes engulfed in rage, bellows, "And you better not get in my way, Chase! You better keep yourself locked up inside that lab and keep Sigmund running! Do you understand?"

Chase fumbles for his glasses that he lost when Dr. Morey jumped him. Slapping Chase's face, Dr. Morey repeats his question.

"Yes, I understand," Chase stutters, still scanning the floor for his glasses.

Shoving Chase towards the door, Dr. Morey marches back to his desk. Pulling out his pocket watch, he crushes it with a menacing fist. His knuckles, ghost white, crack like twigs beneath menacing boots. Finding his glasses, Chase quickly picks them up.

"Oh no," Chase mumbles. Both lenses, cracked beyond use, stare up at Chase mournfully.

"Get out of here," Dr. Morey grumbles, fixing his suit, "I'll notify you when the last subject is ready."

"Yes, Dr. Morey."

***

"You need to come with me," Samantha says, her voice cracking. Jim, teeth barred, twists his boot into the stones. They just shot a report in one of the poorest sectors, Fastendom, and Samantha has been endeavoring to get Jim to attend an Orbis Institute Club meeting with her.

"Why would I want to go there?" Jim retorts, his words sharp. He avoids Samantha's gaze. She has a way of hypnotizing people with her pretty blue eyes.

"It could lead into a great story. Look, it's going to be a celebratory meeting. You only have to attend this one. For Mendacium News."

"I don't want to." Jim, growing more and more bitter, has found himself losing his patience with Samantha. She is obsessed with the Orbis Institute and has made it her mission to convert Jim into a loyal patron. He loathes that. Looking at her from the corner of his eyes, he scoffs. She is an ugly bastard beneath that perfect skin of hers. Worst of all, he has noticed an increase of political and influential people sleeping over at her place. Sure, Jim may have slight neurosis making a concerted effort to drive by Samantha's home at night, but he needs to fuel his hate for her. It's a diabolical addiction. He doesn't know where it came from or how it grew into this, but he hates her. He hates everything about her.

"Come on, Jim," Samantha pleads, grabbing Jim's shoulder, "I know we have our differences, but this could benefit us both. Look, maybe you can ask people questions—"

"I don't want to."

"Jim, it's one time. It won't kill you—"

"I don't want to."

"Jim, I want you there. You have to be there."

"Why?"

"Because there'll be... there'll be," Samantha pauses, "there'll be people there you can question accusingly and maybe get those answers you want so desperately." Samantha, of course, has no intention of allowing Jim to ask any questions, at least not questions that may jeopardize her career or reputation among the elites, but if she can get Jim to change his mind on his stubborn convictions, maybe he won't be such a thorn in her side.

Looking up at her, his eyes cold, Jim searches Samantha's face. A moment of weakness overtakes him. "Fine," he mutters, "I'll go, but I'll hate every second of it."

***

Fixing her hair, Harriet pesters Dr. Morey about how she looks. "I hope I look fine. I spent all morning fixing my makeup. Is Samantha out there? I do say if people compare me to her, I'll look hideous. Damn beauty queen. Dr. Morey, do you think I look fine? There's no mirror back here. I..."

Grumbling, Dr. Morey, replies, "You look fine." For an ogre, that is, he thinks to himself. Of course, he expected nothing less than being stuck with Harriet in a cramped, backstage room. She has a knack for chattering far too obnoxiously about frivolous things. Once Dr. Morey can hear their cue over the speakers in the corner of the room, he will be more than glad to walk out on stage. The Orbis Institute Club, full of expectant faces, listens to its president give an introductory speech for their special guests. Filling the small theatre room that is no longer used for musicals like it once was, the Orbis Institute Club members murmur amongst themselves who they think the special guests are. Guesses ranged from the original prototype to Dr. Hartford. Only a few mentioned the name Dr. Morey, but no one really expected him to be here. He is always busy.

Smiling, the Orbis Institute Club president, an attractive female with an hourglass figure, pauses for effect. The suspense in the room heightens. Reaching her hand towards right stage, she declares, "Give Dr. Walsh and Dr. Morey a warm greeting!" Erupting in applause, the audience of about a hundred people whoop with excitement. Most of them have never met the one and only Dr. Morey. Of course, most of them have never met Harriet either, but no one really cares about Harriet. Taking a seat behind Dr. Morey, who stands at center stage with a microphoned podium at his disposal, Harriet smiles awkwardly, still fretting internally over her hair and makeup. Raising his hand in the air, Dr. Morey hushes the crowd. He scans the audience.

So many different faces spot the full theatre. Samantha, sitting beside miserable Jim, beams with joy. Her eyes are wide. She cannot believe that she is sitting in the front row, so close to Dr. Morey himself. Jim, holding back his complaints, just wishes he could wring Samantha's neck for bringing him here. A couple of rows behind them, hand in hand, Titus and Greta sit together. Smiling from ear to ear, Greta nudges Titus while pointing at Dr. Morey like a movie star. Politely smiling back, Titus wriggles in his seat. If it weren't for Greta, he'd probably be somewhere else, but Greta insisted, and he can hardly say no to her cute smile. In the far back, almost late, Rob lounges in his chair with a voluptuous woman wrapped in his arm. He has seen Dr. Morey before, no need to get excited. A few rows in front of him, taking notes like a true professional, Destiny looks expectantly at Dr. Morey for words of wisdom, pieces of knowledge to muse over later. Surrounding and between these notable faces are enforcers, poor, wealthy, and basic faces of all varieties. They all wait for Dr. Morey's words of brilliance.

"Good evening, everyone," Dr. Morey greets the crowd with a toothy grin. "I'm delighted to finally meet the institute's most loyal supporters. It is my pleasure, no, it is my honor to have the chance to speak to you all today." His large frame commands the stage. His strong arms emphasize his words with a wave of the hand or finger in the air. Dr. Morey has practiced this speech for hours. He perfected every motion and inflection. "As Orbis Institute's patrons, I'm sure all of you understand how monumental tomorrow is, not only for the institute, but also for Orbis as a whole. The final subject, being conditioned by our most prestigious scientist Dr. Hartford, will be completed." The crowd murmurs. Smiling, Dr. Morey nods his head, "I know, it is incredible. We have come a long way. Today, I would like to express Orbis Institute's principles. The ideals that have been our North Star for hundreds of years. The ideals that still stand today." Clearing his throat, he scans the crowd. Pause for effect.

"Enlightenment. Beautiful enlightenment. That is our first principle. Truth is the most important entity this world of ours has. However, the pursuit of truth, the endless philosophizing over truth, or even the discovery of truth, is meaningless. Of course, these steps are necessary, but on their own, they are empty cisterns. No. The most important experience is enlightenment. Enlightenment makes truth reality. The moment I or anyone else is enlightened is the moment Orbis has grown in value. Every step Orbis Institute takes is to further our enlightenment. We crave truth. We hunger for truth; it is our bread and butter. It is our nourishment. We hope, no, we know here at Orbis Institute that one day all of Orbis will be enlightened. That is not a fantasy or some wishful dream. It is truth. We truly believe the Sigmund Project, our most precious project ever, will enlighten generations to come escorting Orbis into a prosperous future, a future no longer wallowing in despair. A future no longer bickering over trivial matters. A future full of wealth, robust skyscrapers, and happiness. Is that not what we want?" The audience cheers. "I tell you, this is only possible through enlightenment. Enlightenment! Good thing at Orbis Institute, we are enlightened. We will pave the way to that splendid future.

"Enlightenment, it inevitably leads into our next principle, virtue. When a person is enlightened, he or she has no choice but to act accordingly. The truth begins to convict their inner being. I would dare to say soul, but of course, I'm a man of science. I am not a superstitious mystic." The crowd chuckles. "The mind, yes, the mind, loves to act upon the truth. Therefore, enlightenment gives birth to virtue because there is nothing more virtuous than living out the truth. Of course, the truth can be painful. Surely virtue may seem like a vice at times, but we cannot, by any means, be discouraged. We must stick to our guns. That is why virtue, how grand it is, must be accompanied by integrity. Integrity, our third principle, is the twin brother to virtue. Banded arm in arm with virtue, integrity will push through the driest desert, the most harrowing thunderstorm, or the most troublesome war. Integrity does not falter. It strengthens a person. It turns legs of jelly into marble pillars. At Orbis Institute, I am proud to say virtue and integrity abide within our DNA. We cannot eat or breathe without virtue being in every bite and integrity being in every exhale. We study, test, experiment, learn, and delve deeper into our research despite the cost because it is virtuous to do so, and we have the integrity to march forward. I would have it no other way. I could not. I am enlightened, after all. To be a coward, to stumble in my morals, would be a disgrace. It would go against the very grain of who I am. No. I, along with everyone, must be virtuous. Must be, at all costs, full of integrity. We cannot have it any other way.

"Of course, these three principles all aid one very delicate entity: life itself. Yes, life. That is our fourth and final principle. Life is far too precious to ignore. It must be bolstered, trimmed, and cared for by utilizing the other three characteristics. Able to crumble with one wrong move or one negligent blow, life is always in a state of instability. Never, in all of history, has life been thoroughly civilized. War, disease, lies, wickedness, religion, reckless philosophy, and several other wretched devices created by man and nature alike have ravaged life. At Orbis Institute, as we grow in the previous ideals, we promise a stable life. It will be the product of perfection. It will, of course, be the product of enlightenment, the product of virtue, the product of integrity. One day, one glorious day, I promise a perfect world. Just walk the path Orbis Institute is paving, and you, too, will see the light at the end of the tunnel. Together, enlightened, we can make Orbis a shining city on a hill. Thank you." Erupting into applause, the audience stands to their feet. Dr. Morey sits down beside Harriet, who is practically in tears from Dr. Morey's enthralling speech. It even managed to get her mind off her appearance. Of course, once everyone returns to the lobby for refreshments, she will fret over her hair again.

"Thank you, Dr. Morey," the president says, her smile genuinely big, "and thank you, club members, for coming to this wonderful event. In the lobby are refreshments. Everyone, at this time, can help themselves. Dr. Morey and Dr. Walsh will, in a moment, be out in the lobby as well. So, if you have any questions or comments to share with them, you will have plenty of time in the lobby to do so. Thank you; you are dismissed."

Chatting over crackers, cheese, wine, and other snacks, Orbis Institute Club members stand in their circles. The poor, in the corner of the lobby, eat much and say little. There isn't much to be said. They just have to wait for things to improve. Discussing, in detail now, vacation ideas, the scientists agree that a week stay at Paddington's most elegant resort would be the best getaway. Bantering about the weather, economics, social events, and other nonessentials, the government officials keep to themselves by the refreshments. The wealthy, drinking most of the wine, brag about their business ventures or their latest purchases. Deep inside, every single one of them is just waiting for Dr. Morey. He is still talking with the president on the stage. Harriet returns, but to her dismay, no one cares to notice. Deflated, she mingles with her fellow government officials, asking them as soon as she can whether her lipstick is the right shade of red. They all lie to shut her up.

"Dr. Morey!" someone cries from the wealthy circle. Sure enough, laughing alongside the president, Dr. Morey proceeds down the stairs towards the lobby. Everyone cheers, their wine glasses tinkling with delight. Raising his hand, Dr. Morey smiles diplomatically.

"Dr. Morey, I'm so glad to see you again," the powerplant owner, Leonard, says with a quirky grin. Shaking Leonard's hand while still moving, Dr. Morey tries to get away as soon as possible.

"Leonard, yes. Glad to meet you."

"Could we discuss the increase in funding I requested several weeks ago?"

"Not right now."

"Sir, we could really—"

"Good day, Leonard." The lights flicker overhead. The crowd hushes. Shocking the air with a stinging noise, the lights flash and return to their normal state. Looking over his shoulder at Leonard, Dr. Morey comments, "Talk to Harriet if you want funding. Don't bother me." Snorting, Dr. Morey thinks to himself, *Good luck with that.*

"Dr. Morey," Samantha calls, sauntering his way with swaggering hips. Her velvet slit dress dances with her tan legs. Dr. Morey's eyes swell with sexual ardor.

"Samantha Pierce," he says. The words roll off his tongue like honey. "What would you like?"

"I was wondering if I could get an interview with you sometime about the Sigmund Project's story. How it all came to be."

"I would love to. I heard you enjoy giving nighttime interviews."

Samantha's cheeks blush, "Well, some may call it my specialty."

"Perhaps tonight at my place. After this celebration, of course."

"It would be my pleasure."

"No need to bring a touchpad. I have my own."

"Certainly."

Squeezing Samantha's shoulder, Dr. Morey says, "See you tonight, then."

Glaring with smoke spewing from his ears, Jim watches from a distance with a full glass of merlot in his pale hand. Fury rages through his veins. *Fuck despair, alright,* he thinks to himself. *Why don't you just fuck the physical form of it?*

Buzzing with mild excitement, the scientists don't bother bidding for Dr. Morey's time. They have all seen him around the institute at one point. Greta, reciting her first time talking with Dr. Morey, tells Titus how brilliant Dr. Morey really is. Titus nods his head, his mind elsewhere. The poor, hoping more than anyone else, for Dr. Morey to pay them some respect, wait patiently for their turn. Certainly, their turn will come. Sometime. After the wealthy is through with him.

Greeting different circles, including the enforcers who are a stoic bunch, Dr. Morey completes his rounds overlooking the poor in the corner. Indeed, a slight oversight. Certainly not intentional. Or that's what the impoverished hope. Their time will come once they are enlightened, or so they believe. After discussing business with the scientists, he escorts Samantha to his sports car, giving everyone a hardy farewell. They all cheer, raising their empty glasses. They are all a little tipsy. All except Jim, who hasn't taken a sip from his merlot yet.

Chapter 12

"Today is the day," Chase mumbles to himself as he walks to work. The same sign, worn down by the elements, still screams the same message.

WHAT THE HELL ORBIS?!

"I don't know," Chase mutters to himself, keeping his head low. "What the hell am I doing?" Chase asks himself. Oliver, odd but loving Oliver, pleaded for Chase not to lay a hand on the final subject. He seemed convinced that Chase would go through with it, but he asked for him to spare her before Chase had to leave. Marching forward mechanically, Chase considers staying home. He doesn't want to go through with it, but the Orbis Institute ingrained their methods into his very DNA. He feels like he's enslaved to their practices.

Preparing the lab for the final subject, Chase listens to "Inventions and Sinfonias" with a grim look wreaking havoc on his face. Mechanical, every action is mechanical. Every effort, a force of habit, seems to be coming from another spirit. It feels like a terrible apparition has possessed him. Groaning, his conscious won't settle, but laying the scalpel in its place, Chase won't listen either.

What am I doing? he thinks to himself.

"Dr. Hartford," a low voice rumbles. Turning, Chase acknowledges Dr. Morey with a simple head nod. He has nothing to say. "Are you ready to make history?" Wearing a purple suit with gold buttons and a tie, Dr. Morey dressed himself in an unusual fashion. His shoes, polished, are gold with diamond studs. He even applied gel to his coarse hair.

"Are you attending a party?" Chase asks, stifling a chuckle.

Frowning, Dr. Morey clears his throat and says, "I have another interview with the Mendacium News after this procedure is over. I thought it would be best if I dressed in the most luxurious outfit I have."

"Looks like something Samantha would approve of."

"I'm certain she would," Dr. Morey growls. "Remember Dr. Hartford, I want you to be quick. Don't dawdle. I'll have a pair of eyes on you at all times."

"What do you mean?"

"I gave orders to some of your colleagues to make sure you behave normally."

"You don't trust me?"

"Quite frankly, not like I used to."

"Well," observing his laboratory, Chase nods, "I think I'm ready. I'll be on my way and let the future commence."

"That's the spirit."

Lowering into the depths of hell, Chase trembles. The elevator, whining, knows today is the day. *What will the subject look like? How old will it be? What will its eyes look like?* Racing, his mind burns through a thousand questions. Sweat oozing from his pores lathers his body. His thin black hair, speckled with white spots, looks like it got rained on. Rubbing his eyes, Chase sees everything around the edges of his vision like a blur. *If only I had my glasses.* He couldn't get a replacement pair soon enough for today. It won't disenable him, but it will force him to be more cautious. Lurching to a halt, the cab's jaws open. Stepping into the viridescent glow, Chase shudders. A draft chills his skin. Goose flesh overtakes his arms. Taking a breath, Chase presses forward.

The howling vents sound like werewolves coming to life. The flickering green lights cast ghastly shadows on the walls. Slinking through the formidable corridors, Chase keeps his head low. He enters the Subject Reserve hallway. The stainless steel door, duller than usual, stares at Chase with the same emptiness in Chase's gut.

"Oh, God forgive me," Chase whispers. His conscience, weighing heavy on his mind, makes his feet feel like lead. He could refuse. He could run off with the subject and return tonight for the final triumph. He could, but fear, still containing the new fire in his eyes, warns him not to be rash.

"Dr. Hartford," Dr. Afreet, wearing a white coat, greets Chase, putting out his hand. Shaking it, Chase avoids Dr. Afreet's eyes. He says nothing. "I will be waiting in the Dismemberment room. Do not dawdle with the subject."

"Yes, Dr. Afreet," Chase replies, his voice staggering.

"Get going."

Nodding, Chase marches forward. He can't rebel. He can't refuse. People are watching. He sees another familiar face by the Subject Reserve door. Destiny.

"May I enter?" Chase asks coldly. Solemn, Destiny doesn't reply. She nods towards the card scanner. Running his card by the scanner, Chase listens to the steel door unlock, just like a prison cell. Destiny, turning towards Chase, watches him wander into the reserve with his back slouched over by shame. On each side of the aisle that Chase walks through are large glass containers. Ventilation systems, like saw blades, set evenly apart, dominate their ceilings. They all hum in unison like an army unit. Sitting in the center of the cylinder containers are circular channels. Orbis Institute's mush, like feed for pigs, gets poured into the troughs two times a day by a fountain that the channels surround. In the corners are grates intended for waste. All the containers are empty. His subject is on the upper floor. Trudging up the spiral stairs at the end of the aisle, Chase keeps his eyes fixed on his shoes.

A sign at the top of the stairs hangs over the stairwell: AGES 0 TO 12

The end closest to the stairwell has hundreds of small pods created for babies and small children. Lit by heat lamps, the egg-shaped capsules have vents at their backs. Tubes, like tentacles, hang from the capsules' ceilings. One for the mouth, some to check for vitals, and one for sanitation. Chase grimaces. Catching his eye, something polka-dotted sits behind one of the capsules. Leaning over, he takes a closer look. It's a pacifier. A green polka-dotted pacifier. Sniffling, Chase ignores it. He doesn't want to think about it. Beyond the egg-shaped capsules are smaller containers like the ones from the first floor. Swallowing a lump in his throat, Chase sees the container number designated for his subject. Container 73. He pulls out his card and swipes. The glass door slides open. Inside, curled in a ball shivering, is the subject.

"I'm here to get you," Chase says dryly. The strength in his voice completely disintegrated. Coiling into a tighter ball, the subject mewls. "Please come," Chase half-whimpers. His face is entirely devoid of color.

"No," the subject squeaks timidly like a mouse.

"Please."

"No."

Quivering, Chase doesn't know what to do. Looking around the facility, he closes his eyes. Two deep breaths. One. Two. Proceeding deeper into the container, Chase closes the door behind him, making sure not to lock it. Churning, the bile in his stomach bubbles. He doesn't want to be here.

"Subject 5,781 of eleven years, please come," Chase says, trying to regain his composure.

"No," the subject replies, shoving its face deeper into its legs. Its simple gray tunic, pulled taut around its knees, presses against the subject's face. Its hair, a brown, knotted mess, hangs over its bony shoulders.

"Please, I don't want this to be difficult."

"I said no!" the subject squeals.

Wetting his mouth, Chase looks around the container. It's empty. Destiny still stands by the steel door.

"Ok," he whispers, sitting by the subject with his head against the glass wall. He assumes a posture he is used to in Oliver's cell. A minute of silence hangs in the thick air. The only thing able to be heard is the vents humming. Stifling a cry, the subject sobs softly. Its cracked feet twitch.

Clearing his constricted throat, Chase whispers, "What's your name?"

The crying stops. The subject sniffles. No reply.

"What's your name?"

"Mary Friedman," the subject whispers, its voice choked by the tunic.

"That's a lovely name."

"Thank you."

"Do you have parents?"

"I did."

"What were their names?"

"Axel and Lucinda."

"Do you miss them?"

"Yes."

Nodding, Chase forges more questions. He's not used to this. He's not used to this weird sentiment he's experiencing. Looking over at the subject, he sees it beginning to relax. Its face is still hidden. He's glad about that. He's scared to look into its eyes.

"What do you enjoy doing?"

"I have a doll at home I like to play with."

"Oh, really?"

"Yeah," sprawling out its legs slowly, the subject keeps its head low so that its hair serves as a barrier between Chase and its face, "I named the doll Sunny."

"With an 'O' or a 'U'?"

"A 'U.'"

"Why?"

"Because she's always smiling. Every day is sunny for her," the subject says, pulling at a knot in its matted hair. "Not always easy or enjoyable, but sunny."

"Sunny," Chase whispers. He smiles, looking over at the subject who is beginning to pull its hair behind its ear. "I like it." Giggling, the subject peers at Chase with only its nose and mouth, peeking from behind its hair.

"You do?"

"Absolutely."

Smiling, the subject tucks the rest of its hair behind its right ear. It looks up at Chase with big brown eyes. Losing his breath, Chase feels his chest burn. It ignited with guilt that sears his heart. He swallows a lump of condemnation lodged in his throat.

The subject—no, it's—it's a girl. A beautiful little girl.

"Are you ok?" Mary asks, her voice soft. Chase nods, avoiding her gaze. Pins and needles prick his fingers. Blazing, Chase's cheeks feel like they are going to melt. Another big breath. Chase looks at the glass door. He looks around the facility. He takes another breath.

"I'm ok," he croaks.

"What's your name?" Mary asks, her face crusty with dried tears.

"Chase Hartford."

"I like your name, too."

"Thanks."

Looking at the door, Mary's smile fades. She shudders like a chill ran down her spine.

"You're not going to make me take this off?" she asks, pinching her tunic.

"Of course not." That's not entirely true. Chase knows that every subject has its tunic removed before entering the Grim Reaper. Shaking his head, Chase doesn't want to bother with that right now. The thought only worsens the guilt.

"Good."

"Why do you ask?"

"A couple of men in white coats made us girls take them off."

Chase can't imagine what for.

"Why did they make you do that?"

Trembling, her bottom lip dribbles with saliva. Horror sweeps across her eyes. Hugging herself, she stares at the floor.

"Did they tell you why you were supposed to take off your tunic?"

"They," Mary stutters, trying her best not to cry, "they didn't say. They just touched us. They poked us. I—I—I didn't want them to."

"Where did they touch you?" Chase asks. He feels another rush of heat surge through his body. Pointing at her waist, she quakes. Anger, something Chase has experienced before, rushes his face.

"Damn perverts," he growls. Mary stares at him with scared eyes. "Sorry," Chase whispers, trying to contain his rage.

"You don't have on a white coat," Mary says, "you won't do that to me."

"Never."

"Promise?"

"Promise."

Footsteps echo throughout the reserve.

"Shit," Chase mutters. Destiny, speed walking towards container 73, has her lips pursed together with impatient disgust. Mary reaches for Chase's hand; he gives it a gentle squeeze. Standing, he helps Mary to her feet as Destiny marches inside the container. She sets her fists menacingly on her hips. Her small figure made wider.

"Dr. Hartford," she hisses, "are you done fooling around?"

"Yes, Dr. Collins."

"Good. Let's get going then."

"Of course."

Falling silent, Mary holds onto Chase's hand as he leads her down the steps. The industrial size lights suspended on the doom ceiling flicker. A draft solidifies Chase's blood. Even his bones shiver.

Dr. Afreet, waiting outside Dismemberment, gives Chase a glowering stare. "How long does it take someone to grab a subject?" he asks harshly, observing Mary and how she huddles close to Chase's side. He swears. "Why, don't get attached to the wretch. It's just a damn animal."

Chase doesn't say anything. Mary looks up at Chase, her big brown eyes searching for comfort. He doesn't look back. He stares into dead space, terrified.

"Oh, for god's sake," Dr. Afreet grumbles, yanking Mary from Chase's grasp.

Snapping out of his trance, Chase retorts, "Be gentle!"

Destiny scoffs with her fists on her hips. She steps back towards Subject Reserve to shut the door. Dragging Mary, who is kicking and screaming, into Dismemberment, Dr. Afreet reaches for a pair of scissors sitting on a nearby tray. Running inside, Chase watches him cut away at Mary's tunic. Giant tears roll down her crimson cheeks.

"You promised! You promised!" she wails, her eyes meeting Chase's, wrenching his heart like a tornado. His conscience screams. Her eyes burrow deep into his spirit, exposing every ugly sin. His heart is raw. It feels pulverized. Welling up with tears, his eyes can't see clearly. Mary's big brown eyes are a murky pool of mud.

"You are useless," Dr. Afreet mutters, throwing the tunic to the side. Punching a few commands into the motherboard, Dr. Afreet opens the Grim Reaper like a mechanical tomb. Heaving Mary, a sobbing mess, into the beastly thing, he locks her in place.

"Chase! Chase! Chase!" Mary cries as the Grim Reaper closes.

"Are you going to do anything?" Dr. Afreet asks, "It's your special day."

The grief chokes him with tears. The paralyzing fear has diffused through every limb. He wants to move, but he just can't seem to do it. He can't seem to do anything.

"You're a disgrace," Dr. Afreet growls, punching commands into the motherboard. Awaking, the Grim

Reaper howls. Clearing his eyes, Chase gazes at the Grim Reaper's face mask, and he sees Mary's eyes. Her large eyes are full of terror. Compassion shatters Chase's heart. He can hardly stand it. The Grim Reaper, a murderous invention, howling louder and louder, sucks the life out of Mary's eyes. He listens to its crude music. He hates it like nails to a chalkboard. Her blank eyes are like glass as they slip into a vacuum. Punching in more commands, Dr. Afreet grabs one of the hundreds of carts in the room and rolls it behind the Grim Reaper. Sorting through the organs, bones, limbs, and other salvageable items, the wretched invention spits containers into a chute. Organizing the cart within a minute, Dr. Afreet wheels it over to Chase who holds onto the Grim Reaper for dear life.

"Dr. Hartford," he calls.

"What?" Chase croaks.

"Your cart is ready."

Shoving Dr. Afreet out of the way, Chase replies, "Her name was Mary. Mary Friedman."

"It's subject 5,781."

"When I revive her, she's being called Mary."

Dr. Afreet frowns. "This is just the process of evolution," he replies, "adapting to new circumstances and growing stronger. That's the only way we can survive. The only reason Orbis is here today."

"Go to hell, Afreet," Chase hisses, wheeling the cart into the corridor.

"I'll see you there."

"No," Chase says, stopping in between the doorposts, "no, you won't."

Making his way to his laboratory, Chase tries his best to ignore Titus, who sits in the corner. His eyes are watching steadily. Chase turns on "Inventions and Sinfonias." He organizes Mary's dismantled body. Damning up the tears just waiting to explode, Chase prepares the solution tub.

"I'm sorry, Mary," he whispers as he sanitizes the metal basin with a white cloth, "Oliver, forgive me."

Turning the valve, Chase watches the faucet gurgle then burst forth with crimson fluid. Giving the tub time to fill, Chase prepares the stretcher. Individual slots, forming a crude impression of a human, direct Chase where to put what. "Mary," Chase whispers, "have you ever wondered what's beyond the wall? I have. I've even been told what I could discover."

"Who are you talking to?" Titus asks, his face twisted with confusion.

"Myself," Chase replies. Titus sits back in his chair.

Sputtering, the faucet stops. Water filled the tub. Finished with the stretcher, Chase calls Titus.

"Help me lower it into the tub," Chase says, grabbing the handle on one end. Titus nods, grabbing the other handle. Lowering Mary's dismembered body into the solution, it bubbles as green algae create a thin film on the solution's surface.

"This still—"

"Shut up," Chase says flatly. He wipes his nose. He can't cry. Not here. Unable to be seen through the solution and film, Mary slowly solidifies. The solution, creating the missing sinews, flesh, skin, and other ligaments, pulls her back into one piece. The fluid bubbles as if the liquid is boiling. The once crimson solution is now a dark shade of green.

"Pull her out." Hauling the stretcher out of the fluid, Mary lies still, her brown hair no longer matted. Her skin, silky smooth, wraps entirely around her remade body. She looks the same, but she is far from the same. She sleeps peacefully. Wheeling Mary into Memory Room, Chase rests her on the nearest programmer after slipping a new tunic over her thin body. The programmers are funky-looking beds with helmets that look like they belong to salon drying chairs. Pulling the helmet over Mary's face, he injects a needle into the side of her neck that attaches to the helmet with a tube. Flashing, the tube beside the bed comes to life. Her memory transfer is ready. Her memories that were and will be further manipulated by the Psychology Department. Glancing at the observation window, he sees Dr. Collins watching him. Her focused eyes don't flit.

Chase looks down at Mary, his dark, watery eyes are lit by a strange fire not extinguished by the forming tears. Turning his back towards Destiny, Chase stares at the endless beds. "They are children," he whispers to himself. "What the hell, Orbis?"

"You know it takes a few hours for the memories to be fully downloaded," Destiny says from in between the door jamb.

"I know," Chase says, still hiding his face. "I want to stay here."

"I don't."

"It's not your day."

"Look at me, Dr. Hartford."

Dabbing at his eyes, he smothers the tears. He looks at Destiny.

"Have you been crying?" She asks with a hint of disgust.

"Maybe."

"Dr. Hartford, Dr. Morey told me to keep my eye on you."

"Then stay here."

"I don't want to. I have work to do."

"Then don't."

"Why do you have to be so difficult?"

"You do realize," Chase says, looking around the walls, "that it would have been easier to install cameras down here than to assign people to watch me."

"The institute never installed cameras down here for privacy reasons."

"In case people somehow got the footage and exposed us."

Crossing her arms, Destiny huffs, "The average person doesn't understand our methods, Dr. Hartford. You used to understand that yourself."

"The average person is human. That's why."

"What does it mean to be human, Dr. Hartford?"

Sitting on the bed by Mary, he looks down at her with a smile. Looking back at Destiny, he gives her a warm grin, "Merry freedom."

"What?" Destiny asks, cocking her head to the side.

"To be human means to be free from this rat race we created. The constant scrambling after vain pursuits," Chase chuckles, shaking his head, "to live for something beyond ourselves. Maybe something as absurd as God. Maybe, by chance, a God who lives. Who lives beyond those walls."

"Dr. Hartford, I think you may need a counselor," Destiny says, her tone surprisingly tender. "Don't you see what we are doing here? We are creating people solely dedicated to Orbis. Their only goal will be the future of Orbis. Their only god will be Orbis. If everyone, and I mean everyone, focuses on what we have right here, we will reach the pinnacle of perfection."

"Dr. Collins, have you ever studied history?"

"Not thoroughly, no."

"Have you ever learned about Hitler?"

"A little bit."

"Genghis Khan? The Rape of Nanking? World War I? Osama bin Laden? The 2250 Cyber Panic?"

"What's your point?"

"We have raised empires, created new philosophies, invented new technology, and have sought after enlightenment. We have never perfected ourselves. There's not even an upward trend."

"This will be different. We are hardwiring the subjects to think the way we want them to think. They will know no different."

"How are you going to convince them to care?"

"What do you mean?"

Holding Mary's hand, Chase sighs, "What do you tell a child—"

"Subject. Th—"

"Children. They are children."

Destiny grumbles.

"As I was saying," Chase continues, "what do you tell a child to care about when all they believe in is Orbis?"

"They will learn to advance Orbis. That will be their mission."

"Why should they commit themselves to such a worthless mission?"

"Worthless?"

"Either everything they build up will be torn down, or in the grand scheme of eternity, it will cease to exist. Ultimately, all their effort will be for naught. If any one of them internalizes this mindset, there are only a few possible responses. They can become nihilists, sadists, or depressed. The best-case scenario, for your purposes, is if they ignore the notion of worthlessness and live in blissful denial. As Dr. Morey told me, fuck despair."

"Surely, you don't think saving Orbis is an awful goal?"

"I'm suggesting that there will come the point when your subjects realize that they have sold their souls to the naturalist devil. They will come to find your mission futile and unattractive. The wise will reject it entirely. Sadly, the conformed will kill themselves. That is their destiny." Dumbfounded, Destiny stares at Chase with wide eyes. He says, "I would like to hear your ethics class as well. I'm sure that will go over well once you have gotten rid of any sort of transcendent law. Most likely, one of your subjects will send you through the Grim Reaper to advance Orbis."

"I'm going back to work," Destiny spits, marching into the corridor. She leaves Chase and Mary alone.

"Mary," Chase whispers, clasping her small hand, "we'll soon be free. Oliver will save us. You can trust me. I promise."

Beeping after about three hours, the tube alerts Chase the memory transfer is complete. Disengaging the needle and helmet, he rolls up Mary's sleeves. Chase fills another syringe with a clear fluid. Injecting it into Mary's arm, he waits for a second. Gasping, Mary sucks in a few sharp breaths. Her chest heaves rapidly.

"Easy, easy, easy, Mary," Chase says soothingly, holding Mary's hand. Snapping her head around, Mary looks up at Chase with her glossy brown eyes. The life that used to be there, the lofty dreams she used to hold onto, are gone. Yanking her hand back, she sinks into the bed with her arms crossed. Gently prodding, Chase whispers, "Mary, we must leave here."

"No," she growls.

"Mary," Chase says, sitting on the edge of her bed, "we must go upstairs."

Staring at him with eyes like empty cisterns, she shakes her head vehemently.

"Mary."

"Why?" She retorts with two balled fists, ready to strike. "Why should I?"

"You need to receive your training and certification from the Psychology Department."

"I asked why! Why should I?"

"Why do you think you should?"

Mary, looking clueless, stares at Chase with her mouth agape.

"Why?" Chase repeats.

"For Orbis," she grumbles. Her eyes, narrowed with animosity, burn a hole through the bed.

"Why does Orbis matter?"

"Because..." Mary pauses to think, "because we are here."

"Why do we matter?"

"Because we want to live."

"Just to die all the same?"

Growing red in the face, Mary constricts her fists further, making them dove white.

"We die to further Orbis," she squeals as she sorts through her edited memories.

"Only for Orbis to slip away like sand in an hourglass."

Mary's crimson cheeks pulsate with heat. Her trembling lip stammers a few nonsensical words before a tear creeps down her cheek. Balling, she wraps her hands around her face. Her hair drapes across her cheeks like towels.

"Mary," Chase whispers softly, lifting her into his lap. She doesn't resist. Hugging her, he hums a piece from "Inventions and Sinfonias." Her tears begin to fade as they trickle like a leaky faucet. "Mary," Chase says again once her wail mellowed into a light cry, "Orbis was never meant to stand alone. Its creator had a much grander purpose."

"Purpose?"

"Yes, purpose. We have something to live for. We have something to strive for that will never fade away."

"Never?"

"Never. An eternity drinking from the chalice of life. Always being in the state we were meant to be in."

"How do you know this?" Mary asks, her teary eyes filled with a glimmer of hope. A light at the end of the tunnel filters through the void.

"I have faith. Faith grounded in plausible reason."

Mary nods, a flicker of fire returning to her pretty brown eyes.

"We must go upstairs, however," Chase says. He wishes he could tell Mary his plans, but he fears she may expose them to Destiny or someone else. If anyone discovers what Chase and Oliver have planned for tonight, it will inevitably fail.

"I don't want to."

"I know, but you must trust me."

Hesitating, Mary tucks her hands under her armpits. She huddles near her knees.

"I trusted you before," she whispers, "you promised."

Tearing up, Chase pulls Mary in close so that her ear is near his mouth. He says softly, "I won't freeze this time." Pulling her head back, she searches Chase's eyes. She sees the fire through the lake of tears. Nodding slowly, she wraps her arms around his neck. Picking her up, Chase carries her to the elevator. He moves her past the condescending eyes that fill the hallways. He takes her into the elevator that leads to the Psychology Department.

The excruciating seconds that pass on that elevator feel like hours of torture. Feeling the anxiety rise, the nearly unbearable apprehension, Mary wraps her arms tighter around Chase's neck. Nuzzling her face into his shoulder, she trembles. The elevator comes to a halt at the twenty-ninth floor. Splitting apart like a curtain, the elevator dings. Filled with cubicle rooms, evenly spaced, the floor looks like a high school. Signs strung across the ceiling direct newcomers to their posts. Classroom Area. Analytical Area. Computer Room. Library. Break Room. Data Retrieval Room. Psycho-Analysis Area.

With Mary still in his arms, Chase passes by the oddly identical rooms that look like miniature dormitories. Some professors, volunteering their time from across Orbis, teach classes to the updated subjects. Chase manages to overhear lectures from opened rooms.

"The universe was a product of chance. Our very existence, the odds significantly not in our favor, is an almost unfathomable possibility. Yet, here we stand today. We must make the most of our time here."

"Evolution, as it progressed through time, gave way for highly advanced creatures such as us. Nature, in control of our world, determined our state."

"Of course, morality as a whole is relative. I have as much say over what ethics should be as much as a rat. Although, we should expect that if everyone does what is best for oneself as in the case of ethical egoism, we will live in harmony."

"Remember, as you discover your talents, pursue a career that conforms to those talents. Develop those skills and be the most efficient worker you can. Certainly, seek well-paying opportunities, but don't forget why you're here. You're here to make Orbis better. You're here to give Orbis another step forward."

Walking beyond the Classroom Area, he breaches the Psycho-Analysis Area. White-coated professionals counsel empty-eyed subjects.

"I can't shake the feeling of more," a fair, red-haired boy says.

"There isn't anything more. This is it. Transcendence is a sickness of the brain as Sigmund pointed out years ago. Ignore those silly notions and pursue what Orbis can be. A city on a hill. That is your fate."

Pushing past the Psycho-Analysis Area, concealing his reproach, Chase takes a left towards Destiny's office. Peering from her desk, Destiny spots Chase through her window. She grabs her touchpad and punches in a few more entries. Lowering Mary, Chase whispers, "I'll be back."

Gazing into Chase's eyes, Mary nods absently.

"Subject 5,781, come here," Destiny says from her open office door. In the crook of her arm is the touchpad, ready for another subject to fill out their form.

Mary temporizes, her eyes bouncing between Destiny and Chase. After a minute, Mary gives Chase a lingering look. Nodding his head, Chase mouths, "Go." Obediently, she plods towards Destiny.

"You made the right decision, Dr. Hartford," Destiny says approvingly, "the future will smile upon you."

"I know," Chase replies with deceptive positivity.

Delightfully surprised, Destiny smiles as she takes Mary's arm and leads her into the office. Looking over her shoulder, Mary gazes at Chase. He waves, fighting the pain in his chest. The pain that will soon be satisfied.

Chapter 13

Sitting beside Peter in his green pickup truck, Chase scratches his face. Discursive, he blubbers about how he doesn't have his glasses, about how dark it is, about how impossible it all seems, about the odds not being in their favor, and about anything that could possibly go wrong.

"Hush. Hush," Peter hisses as Chase stammers. "Hush. Do you believe this can work? Do you believe this is a part of your purpose?"

"Of course," Chase murmurs, "but—"

"Do you believe?"

"Yes."

"Then let your worries dissipate. We don't have time to worry. We must focus on the goal at hand — to deliver these children from living hell."

"What are you going to do?" Chase asks. It just occurred to him that Oliver never mentioned Peter joining their escape.

"I'll be right behind you guys. I have a couple of tasks at the jailhouse to handle before I flee."

"Bother," Chase mutters, "why me? How did I get roped into all this? I can't believe I signed up for this."

Laughing, Peter playfully slaps Chase on the shoulder, "Dr. Hartford, you don't sign up. You're chosen. Welcome to joy. It sucks all right, but man is it worth it."

Chase chuckles as his face lifts. Sitting back in his polyester seat, he closes his eyes. Oliver, like a radiant sun, beams. His olive skin, tender eyes, and pearly smile look down upon Chase with genuine pleasure. Warmth envelopes him like a hug and spreads across his body. The consternation in his tight chest loosens. Oliver, his savior, will deliver him. He will save the children. Chase believes. Fading like a mist, Oliver's features shift into that of a little girl. Mary, her petite face bragging beautiful brown eyes, gazes at Chase with confident hope. She calls out his name. Planting his feet into the ground, Chase drives his body against Dr. Afreet. Chase claws like a bear. Sitting on a tray, like a shiny amulet, a pair of scissors grab Chase's attention. Usurping Dr. Afreet by his collar, he gets ahold of the scissors. Swearing belligerently, Dr. Afreet tries to push back, but it's too late. The scissors, like a sword, split his sternum with exact precision. His heart implodes as the blood gushes from the cavity. Gratified, Chase looks into Dr. Afreet's eyes. Melting, like a snow cone, Dr. Afreet slips through a grate. In his place stands Dr. Morey, with the scissors lodged sideways across his cardiovascular system. Gasping for air, his ugly face is, for the first time, afraid. Utterly afraid.

"He's alive!" Dr. Morey yells, blood spewing from the corner of his mouth. Chase cocks his head to the side. "He's alive!" More blood spills over his chin. Shaking his head, Chase doesn't understand. "He's alive!"

"Look alive! Alive! Alive!" Peter hollers, shaking Chase awake. Snorting, Chase rubs his weary eyes. "Can't you stay awake for five minutes? Hide in the back. We are soon there." Shuffling into the back seat, Chase rolls onto the floor. The tightness in his chest grows. He feels the jerk of a speed bump. Peter stops for a moment to interact with a guard. He thanks the guard and drives forward. Declining into the garage, Chase can feel his stomach flip flop. The doubts rush his head.

I shouldn't be here. I could flee. I could lie and say I was kidnapped. I could just walk out. I could—I can't. I must commit. I must believe.

Jumping out of the truck, Peter slams the back door. Nearly leaping out of his skin, Chase tumbles out of the truck. His red cheeks glow with embarrassment.

Flitting back and forth, Chase swears there are pairs of eyes everywhere. Every crevice in the wall conceals a camera. Every sound is Dr. Morey coming for blood.

"Oh god," Chase mutters, "oh, god."

"To what god do you plead?" Peter asks, his eyes attentively scanning his surroundings.

"It's a figure of speech."

"A rather odd one, if I must say so myself, unless directed towards God; otherwise, it seems silly." Chase apologizes sheepishly. "All is good. Now, let us proceed forward. I know a way typically guard-free. Here, wear these just in case." Pulling a pair of sunglasses and a crumpled hat from his cargo pants, Peter hands them to Chase. Chase thanks him. Slinking through a narrow door hidden behind several SWAT vans, they pass under a monstrous cobweb. Dimly lit, the corridor whistles ominously. Someone plastered wood planks over the steel doors. All the air vents, there aren't many, have been stripped down so that they are nothing but holes in the floor. A weird sensation tickles the back of Chase's neck. Looking over his shoulder, he catches a glimpse of a shadow—a four-legged shadow skulking this cursed corridor for prey.

"What was this hallway used for?"

"It was where we kept death-penalty prisoners. A waiting room for death."

"It looks like it hasn't been in use for a while."

"No, it hasn't. Well, one room still serves a purpose."

"That is?"

"The execution room itself."

"Never relocated that room?"

"Oh, we have a new execution room for prisoners. The one in this hall," Peter pauses, he stifles a groan, "it's used on disabled children."

"Really?" Chase asks. "I wasn't aware of this."

"Well, Dr. Morey still has his secrets. When the enforcers rounded up the children, any that were disabled beyond reasonable use were disposed of in this very hallway."

"That—"

"Is cruel. Of course, disabled children present no future. They lack social skills, they're dependent on other more capable people, they add no economic benefit, and are, for the most part, just burdens on society. Besides, what type of life can a retard lead that is meaningful? Or so the logic goes."

"Or so it goes," Chase echoes. Did he ever share such beliefs? Surely, he was aware of how far his views could stretch. He, shamefully, would have agreed with that logic. To give children who presented no social gain a chance to live would be preposterous when creating a generation geared towards Orbis, a society whose moral code is simply based around one's own needs.

"That is the very world we must change," Peter says, his voice kept at a hush just in case someone is listening.

"I concur."

Reaching concrete stairs that proceed upward in a rectangular fashion, they tread lightly. Peter warns Chase to keep his face hidden behind Peter's body. Cameras lace the stairwell. Assenting slowly, they remain silent. Bugs scrape the concrete walls, ricocheting off them like a million pebbles. Centipedes dash for the nearest hiding spot as soon as Chase or Peter steps in their general direction. Holding his breath, Chase hates the stench. An odor much like a compost pile fills the stairwell.

"Stop," Peter says, placing his hand against Chase's thumping chest. "I'm going to check the area before proceeding. Wait here." Slipping through a grey door, Peter disappears for a moment. Keeping his breathing steady, Chase tells himself he'll be ok. A minute passes. Chase checks the stairs; the dissent would be easy.

I could run. I could make a quick dash. Maybe Peter was caught. Perhaps this is all for naught. No. No. I must stand my ground.

Returning, Peter waves for Chase. Sneaking through the door, Chase stalks Peter. He keeps as close to him as possible. A couple of guards, oblivious to their surroundings, chat amongst themselves inside what looks like a break room.

"Oliver's cell is in the room three doors down on the left," Peter whispers.

"Right."

Creeping towards the door, Peter peeks through the rectangular window. No one is patrolling the cells. "Coast clear." Nodding, Chase follows Peter through the door. The prisoners, fast asleep, snore loudly.

"Oliver isn't asleep, hopefully," Chase mutters.

"On a night like this? You're funny."

Reaching Oliver's cell, Peter unlocks the door as quietly as possible. Inside, on his knees, Oliver waits. His passionate eyes, focused on heaven, don't even flinch at the sound of the creaking door. Mouthing silent words, he holds his head high. Sweat, noticeable sweat, pools around his brow.

"Oliver," Peter says with urgency, "we don't have time to waste."

Finishing his prayer, Oliver rises to his bare feet. His white jumpsuit, giving off a vanilla scent, makes him look like an archangel. Rubbing his bad eyes, Chase could have sworn he saw Oliver glow again. Just for a second.

"Like a thief in the night," Oliver says, "let us go."

"What are you doing?" Pablo, with a stiff cup of coffee in hand and chew beneath his tongue, squints with baggy eyes. "Peter? Oh, my go—"

Splashing the hot coffee in Pablo's face, Peter blinds him for a second. Pablo gropes for his gun while screaming. Peter, in one fluid motion, twists Pablo's arm. Lunging him into the wall, Peter wraps a powerful arm around Pablo's neck. At this point, the prisoners are awake. Those who can see are cheering.

"Rip him to shreds!"

"Bust his ass!"

"Crush him!"

"Come on! Come on!"

Struggling, Pablo kicks his feet. Throwing himself onto the ground, back first, Peter wraps his legs around Pablo's waist. Unable to breathe, Peter's adversary grapples for his gun again. Peter, with one free arm, steals the gun, sending it across the floor. Amidst the confusion, Chase and Oliver sneak out the same way Chase entered the building. Peter handed his keycard to Chase before the fighting commenced.

Beet red, Chase huffs and puffs as he runs. Sprinting has never come naturally for him. Athletics, in general, has never been his strong suit. Oliver, right behind him, keeps pace.

"What are we going to do about the snipers?" Chase wheezes. The prison's wall, only a hundred feet away, is full of nighttime patrols, their guns ready to kill.

"Just keep running," Oliver replies in between breaths.

With his head low, Chase prays Oliver is right. Seventy feet. Fifty feet. Thirty feet. Glancing at the patrols, Chase realizes they can't see them. It's like he and Oliver are invisible. Looking over his shoulder at Oliver, Chase can still see him. Ten feet. The gate, not wholly closed, remains open wide enough for them to slip through.

"How?" Chase whispers.

Slipping through the gate, they bolt for the institute. The snipers, the patrols, the guards are all completely oblivious. It is as if Chase and Oliver are invisible. A half an hour has passed. Reaching the Orbis Institute, Chase swipes his ID card to get inside. The foreboding jaws open. They're inside.

***

A purple suit with gold buttons strewn across the floor beside a pair of polished shoes sits idly at the foot of a rocking bed. Samantha's famous ruby slit dress peeks out from beneath Dr. Morey's trousers. The lush carpet clothing Samantha's bedroom listens to the moans of two sailors out at sea. Vibrating, Dr. Morey's touchpad chimes.

"My dear," Dr. Morey sighs, looking into Samantha's eyes, "let me check my message."

Samantha smiles smugly with lasciviousness lingering in her entrancing pupils. "Don't take too long."

Leaning across Samantha's bed, Dr. Morey reaches for his touchpad. "Who is messaging me at a time like this?" Picking up his tablet from the nightstand, he takes a quick look. His eyes narrow. "What's he doing?"

"What's wrong?" Samantha asks, sitting up.

"Dr. Hartford entered Orbis Institute. Damn nuisance."

"Can't you worry about that later?" Samantha asks, deliberately yawning so that her arms stretch open wide and her breasts stick out firm and stiff.

"I wish I could, my dear," he replies, "but I can't ignore this." Kissing Samantha, Dr. Morey quickly slips back into his suit and runs out the door with his shoes swinging from one hand and his tablet from the other. Rolling out of bed, Samantha grabs her touchpad.

"Jim, we may have a story," she whispers to herself.

***

Unable to sleep, Destiny tosses back and forth in bed. A horrible nightmare keeps haunting her mind. One moment, she is wandering through the Subject Reserve, and the next, she is in a dark room filled to the brim with fog. It's at this moment the nightmare becomes truly dreadful. Sludge, like quicksand, eats away at her ankles. She calls out for help, she trudges through the muck, but it does no good. She's stuck. Doubling over, she tries to catch her breath, but bones rattle as soon as she does so. An inescapable presence permeates the room. She feels fear course through her veins. Spawning from the sludge, Grim Reapers encircle her. They, like a possessed army, all open at the same time. The terrorizing noise, like a million gas chambers opening for Holocaust victims, grates her ears. It shakes the room. It unsettles the sludge. Crawling from the Grim Reapers are skeletons, bone-white skeletons. Their jaws chatter as if to be laughing. Their arms shiver with excitement. They do this in unison like crazed members of a cult.

Suddenly, something cold shackles her ankles. The sludge thickens and solidifies. Throwing a frenzy, the skeletons chatter and dance around Destiny with deadly delirium. They rattle their bones like maracas, all chattering in unison. Raising her body higher, the sludge eats away at her like a parasite. It swallows her and hardens. Destiny tries to scream, but nothing can come out. She is mute. Drums begin to play in the background. They play the sound of a heartbeat. With every second, the drums quicken. The skeletons, chattering louder and louder, accelerate their dance. With every second, they rattle their bones more passionately. Paralyzed, Destiny feels the sludge creep towards her face. The drums get louder. They get faster. The skeletons are berserk at this point. Beating each other, they rattle and chatter louder and louder. They are mad. They are insane, and with every second, they get louder and faster, louder and faster in one deranged unison.

Suffocating her, the sludge hardens. It encapsulates her in a metal death machine. Destiny panics, unable to breathe. Her heart spikes. The drums cease. The skeletons collapse into a pile of bones. Screaming, the Grim Reaper impales Destiny's heart. Then she wakes. Over and over again, the dream occurs whenever she closes her eyes. Clearing the sweat from her face, she swears under her breath. Getting up, she decides to go to work to, hopefully, get her mind off the Grim Reaper.

***

Hurrying through the eldritch glow, Chase and Oliver head for the Subject Reserve. Exhausted already, Chase is glad they will have a chance to rest. Catching his breath, he pants while unlocking the Subject Reserve door.

"Good job, Chase," Oliver says, patting Chase on the back.

"Thanks," Chase gasps, "you are in great shape for someone who has been in prison."

"I'm always active, that's why," Oliver chuckles.

Unable to grin, Chase merely croaks. Oliver instantly grows somber as they enter the reserve. Thousands of faces, at the sound of someone stepping into their world, peer upward. Hollow eyes, like black holes, stare at Oliver with hopeless disinterest. Hurrying in and out of the reserve, dozens of professionals have pricked and prodded the subjects only to leave again. Why should Oliver be any different? Marching down the aisle with thousands of hurting eyes following his every step, Oliver hunches over like a terrible burden lies on his shoulder. Falling to his knees in the center of the dome-shaped room, he weeps profusely. Embarrassed, Chase keeps his distance, trying his best to hide his shame. Why is Oliver crying? They don't have time to waste. The weeping doesn't stop; Oliver cries bitterly. The tears pool around his knees.

Growing bolder, Chase keeps his head low as he approaches Oliver. He's making a fool of himself. Besides, what practical use is there in crying? Security could be here at any time. Oliver must remain collected for this mission to succeed. Dropping to one knee, Chase whispers sharply, "Oliver, I know these are deplorable conditions, but we mustn't dawdle. Stop crying."

"Get behind me," Oliver rebukes in between sobs. "Look around instead of down."

Taken aback by Oliver's sharp reply, Chase hurries back. Raising his head, fighting the shame, he scans the room. Thousands of eyes, like hollow springs, gush forth with streams of fresh water. The tears clean their cheeks.

They cleanse their dirt-stained faces. Gathering, crowding the glass walls, the children are intrigued by this man of many sorrows. They can empathize with his pain. Standing shakily, Oliver clears his fiery eyes.

"Let the prisoners be set free," Oliver commands. Chase obediently hurries to a keypad by the steel door. Swiping his ID and punching in a ten-number sequence, he enters the code into the system. Hissing, every entrapment and capsule opens. Mixed emotions sweep across the children. Some, too stunned to move, hesitate. Others, much more cynical, scoff and are sure it's another test. They wait to see what will happen to the elated children who have burst out the doors as soon as they opened. Like a herd of sheep, the delirious children run to Oliver. They frolic, dance, shout, and chatter. Those older than thirteen try to act more mature by clapping hands and giving each other hugs. The stairs clatter with small feet. The young ones, under ten, are entirely submerged in joy. Spinning, laughing, tugging at Oliver's clothes, they shout obnoxiously. They're free. Truly free!

Smiling, Oliver presses through the crowd to those who remain inside their entrapments. The little ones, excited, chase each other around Oliver's legs. A wave of elated children follows Oliver as he approaches a group of teenage boys.

"Will you follow me?" Oliver asks, a few tears still lingering in his eyes.

Huffing, the dominant one of the group puffs out his muscular chest. He plants his feet like a linebacker. Crossing his arms, he says, "I don't trust anyone."

"Except yourself?"

The four boys behind their leader look at him, expecting a response. He gives none. Just a stubborn lip sealed shut.

"To stay here is to die," Oliver says.

"It's a test," the dominant one retorts. Looking over his shoulder, he eyes down the others. "It's a test I tell you."

"Who will you listen to?" Oliver asks the others. They don't reply. Stiller than stones, they stare at their leader with fear ceasing their hearts. Sheepishly, one boy, to the left of the dominant one, tries to step towards Oliver.

Putting out his fist, the dominant one growls, "Don't even think about it. This is for your own good." Nodding, the boy scuttles back into his position. The other three don't even budge.

Sighing, Oliver leaves the boys behind. In another entrapment are two girls, no older than fifteen, holding hands. They shiver, and they shake.

"Will you follow me?" Oliver asks, his voice gentle. The girls shake their heads. "Why?"

"We're afraid," they remark, backing farther into the cell.

"What are you afraid of?"

"We remember the outside world," the smaller of the two whispers. "They're savages. Brutal savages."

"Is that what I look like to you?"

"We don't know you. We can't trust you."

"He's gonna save us!" an adolescent squeals.

"Didn't you listen?" the larger of the two girls snaps. "There is nothing to be saved from. We are born here, and we die here. I'd rather stay here where I know it's safe."

"It's not safe," says the boy.

"Safer than a stranger."

"He's a friend." Done trying to reason with a child, the larger girl falls quiet.

"To stay is to die," Oliver says. "I'll lead you to life." The girls shake their heads.

"The door remains open," Oliver says, heading for other hesitant children. Chase, forcing a smile past his anxiety, pushes through the kids playing with his shoes. A million questions, from left and right, bombard him.

"God of Oliver," Chase prays, "give me the strength to persevere."

"How old are you?"

"Why are you so ugly?"
"You stepped on my toe!"
"I had a dog."
"Told you to knock it off, Johnny!"
"Do you work here?"
"Do you have a pet?"

Not responding, Chase proceeds up the steps fighting for his balance as a stampede of adolescent boys sprint for Oliver. Gripping the railing, Chase takes a deep breath. He needs to find Mary, to assure her he kept his promise this time. Walking past the wailing babies whose capsules have disengaged and opened, Chase rubs his temples.

"Later. Later," Chase mumbles. Container 73, only a few feet away, is bare except for one little girl. Sitting, she scans the room for a familiar face.

"Mary!" Chase calls, shoving children aside as they scurry by his legs. Perking, she looks around with urgency. "Mary! Mary!" Chase hollers. Spotting him, Mary jumps to her feet. She bolts out of the container. Reaching the door, Chase catches Mary as she leaps into his arms.

"You actually are here!" Mary shouts with happy tears washing over her tender cheeks.

"I told you I'd be back." A shrill whistle echoes throughout the room. In the center of the reserve, standing on a bucket, is Oliver with his arms outstretched. Huddling around him, the children hush themselves. Chase carries Mary down the steps. Even the babies have fallen silent.

"Children!" Oliver cries, his voice swelling with passion, "Today is the day you will all be set free! I will take you beyond the wall to my Father's land!" The adolescents cheer. The teenagers whisper amongst themselves.

"We have been told there is nothing beyond the wall," a dead-eyed thirteen-year-old girl cries. Her pale blue eyes, glazed over like her peers, can't fathom there being anything other than Orbis. Her memories, just like the others, don't recall such tales.

"You have been told a lie. Do you know who built those walls?"

"Adam," a boy cries out.

"Indeed. Why did he build those walls?"

"To protect Orbis from the outside," the thirteen-year-old girl says.

"What lies outside Orbis that is so deadly?"

The kids, steadily getting louder, blurt out all the fearsome plagues, beasts, elements, and monsters that rule the ruthless wasteland. Raising his hand above the chatter, Oliver draws the children's attention back to him.

"What is deadlier than those things?" Oliver asks. The kids blink absent-mindedly. With a patient smile, Oliver says, "I tell you, anyone who tries to persuade people to cross such a dreadful wasteland for an inconceivably perfect world is truly the deadliest foe."

"Why is that?" the thirteen-year-old girl asks. Her eyebrows furrowed in confusion.

"Because he asks that you might die in order to live. The very contradiction itself spits in the face of Orbis. It can't, nor will it ever, understand. That's what the walls are for. They are meant to keep whatever threatens Orbis's comfort and stability an arm's length away. Orbis's leaders, researchers, and brightest never traversed the wasteland to discover the truth!" Oliver cries, tears forming in his eyes again, "They heard, they felt and knew inexplicably that there was more beyond the walls, but the wasteland. Oh, the dreadful wasteland, it kept them from exploring. So, they noted that no one should ever leave Orbis. They noted that no one could leave Orbis. Until they eventually concluded that only Orbis remains. This conclusion nearly destroyed this generation." The lofty words, surpassing the adolescents' understanding, still did not fall void on their ears. Their eyes brightened. A fire lit behind their once dead pupils. Waxing stronger, the teenagers straighten their backs. A new life rushes their nostrils. They, too, have fire behind their eyes.

Light, leaking out of Oliver's pores like sweat, brightens his body like a distant star. "I promise there is more beyond those walls. Beyond the wasteland. I promise freedom! I promise salvation from this cursed city! I promise you a future!"

Shouting in unison, the children raise their battle cry. Chase can see it now. He can see the faith Oliver praised so highly, and it is beautiful.

Chapter 14

A couple of minutes out from Orbis Institute, Dr. Morey sees a parade of children trumping through the main road between Paddington and Boltstock. Their leader, a dark-skinned man in white linen, marches forward with his head high.

"No! No!" Dr. Morey yells. Swerving onto a small street on the left, he curses. He doesn't want to ruin his life's work with one foolish attempt to stop this escape. Speeding for the institute, Dr. Morey hurries inside.

Downstairs, helping keep order, Chase directs the children to the emergency exit. In the back of the line with infants, young adolescents, and weak-legged children in their arms, the teenagers filter through the exit as quickly as possible. The Subject Reserve, draining empty besides a few hundred children still confident that they can't trust Oliver, flickers. The lights threaten to blow. Heavy footsteps knock against Chase's ears. He turns around with Mary sitting on his shoulders. At the end of the hallway, Dr. Morey comes to a halt, his cold eyes set on Chase. Chase's heart jumps. The lights black out. The whirring discontinues, and the children freeze for a moment.

"Keep going!" Chase hollers, locking his fear inside his queasy gut. Dr. Morey's shadow slinks away towards the elevator. The eldritch glow returns slowly as the green lights come to life. The backup generator turned on. Most of the lights are still off, and hardly anything runs.

"Are we going to make it?" Mary asks. Her voice shudders.

"I'm sure," Chase says, forcing a smile past his anxiety. Stimulated by the power outage, the teenagers hustle through the exit faster. Escorting the final teenager through the exit, Chase marches in the back to make sure none straggle behind.

Throwing his touchpad against the elevator door, Dr. Morey swears belligerently. No power and no service. Waiting for the elevator to make it to ground level, he clenches his fists to relieve the tension he feels throughout his body. He knew Chase was going mad, but he wasn't aware to what extent. He never imagined that Chase would actually initiate an uprising. He's trying to overthrow everything the institute has strived for all in one night. It's impossible. Shaking his head, Dr. Morey swears at the elevator, demanding it go faster. Dinging, the doors open. "Finally," he mutters. Running through the halls, his 270-pound figure shaking the whole floor, Dr. Morey reaches the main lobby. Behind the counter, near the main entrance, is a lever. Yanking on it, Dr. Morey spins around. The giant painting, ten feet by ten feet, splits apart. Behind it is a tunnel that leads to the outside. A small lot behind Orbis Institute's guard wall holds in it an arsenal of flares and rockets.

"This better work," Dr. Morey grumbles. Grabbing a lighter from his pocket, he lights the rockets. Angled in such a way that they shoot not into the building or the wall, the rockets fly through a small gap between the lot's roof and the wall. Picking up two flare guns, he quickly fires off a couple of flares as well. The exploding rockets sparkle like fireworks but thunder like foreboding storm clouds. The roar rips through the children. Panic would have swept them away if it weren't for Oliver holding their attention. They had a new leader.

Diving out of bed, Harriet hits her head against her dresser. Moaning, she rubs her throbbing skull. Outside her window, fireworks shower Orbis Institute with an array of colors.

"What is going on?" she asks, still rubbing her tender scalp. Trying to turn on the lights, she can't. "The power must be out." Fretting over where her shoes are, she eventually finds them under her bed. Almost rolling down the steps, she heads for her van.

Watching the tail end of the children flee the institute, Destiny hops out of her running vehicle, dumbfounded. Frazzled, her blond hair stands on end. Her mouth hangs unhinged. "Impossible. This can't be." Running inside as quickly as possible, she nervously proceeds down the elevator. "Impossible," she mutters over and over again. Lurching, the elevator doors creak open. Sprinting through the swamp-like corridors, she runs into the Subject Reserve, her face whitewashed. She stands in an empty, black abyss.

"Impossible," she mutters.

"Who's there?" a loud voice asks. Destiny shivers and glances over her shoulder. A shadow with four other shadows behind it encircles her. Pivoting on her heels, she sees other shadows creep around her.

"Dr. Collins," Destiny squeaks like a frightened mouse.

"The devil herself," the dominant shadow hisses.

"No. No. I helped you," Destiny sputters, unable to think straight. Her heartbeat drums behind her ears, and blood rushes her heated face.

"Fuck off! I help myself. This is a test, isn't it?" the dominant shadow asks with his brusque voice.

"No. There's been a mistake."

"I'm sure there has been. I bet at any moment, you and your team are going to be here just to dismantle us again."

"Orbis is the future. Orbis is all there is. This was to free you," Destiny pleads, her hands up like she's surrendering.

The dominant shadow pauses and cackles. Destiny's heart is ripping at her chest like a jackhammer. "I am free. Free to do as I will. This is some kind of test. I'm sure of it. But this one, I'm going to enjoy."

"What are you talking about?"

"In order to be like you, we must kill like you."

"That's nonsense."

"Is it?" the dominant shadow retorts, drawing nearer. Something rests in its hand. Something sharp and serrated.

"Of course, what about Orbis? Do what's right."

Laughing, the dominant shadow mocks her, "Do what's right? Oh, hell, that's a good one. Morality is relative. I thought that's what you taught me?"

Beating faster, Destiny's heart is on the verge of exploding. She spins around like a tornado. The shadows are encroaching upon her. "Please, look. It doesn't have to be like this."

"We're all going to die. This is it. That's how we must think now. You made us aware of that. We passed the test, didn't we?" the dominant shadow antagonizes.

"You don't understand! Please! This isn't how it has to end!"

"But you said it does."

"No! Please! Wait! Wait! Wait!" Destiny wails as a couple of pieces of serrated glass cut her skin.

"Let's check those organs, bitch!" the dominant shadow bellows. Then all the shadows are upon her.

At a jogging pace, Oliver leads his army of children to the giant closed gate. His eyes, however, do not waver. Seeping through every tissue in his body, courage keeps his feet moving. The children, likewise, are the same. They don't understand, but they know Oliver is the only one who can save them. In the distance, the group can hear the rumble of SWAT vans. The law enforcement got Dr. Morey's message.

Above the chaos, Rob sits on the edge of another bed with his lady friend sleeping soundly despite the ruckus. The curve of her naked back curls towards the pillow she holds onto. Unable to sleep, Rob stares out the window. He heard the explosions but didn't pay much attention to them. Even the parade of children hardly strikes his interest. A sort of despondency chills his heart. What concern should he have for Orbis Institute, anyway? What difference does it all make in the grand scheme of things? Looking over at his lady friend, he sighs. He has everything he needs anyway.

A couple of blocks away, an apartment complex towers over the road. Marching by it, Oliver whistles to himself. Near the top floor, two intimate souls sleep together. Titus, kissing Greta's neck, hears the whistling. Again, he tries to check what's going on outside. Earlier, he heard the thunderous noise of rockets, but Greta told him not to worry about it. Titus also swore he heard SWAT vans firing to life, but Greta only pulled his head closer to her mouth. As Titus tries to crane his neck towards the window, Greta pulls him towards her breasts.

She whispers, "My darling, don't worry about it. I told you that you're worried about nothing. We'll reap the benefits. Now, please, let us enjoy this moment."

"You're right. I'm just overly anxious," Titus mumbles as Greta's breasts consume his mouth.

Looking left and then right, Chase reassures himself they can do it. He knows they can make it. The sound of SWAT vans, however, has rattled his bravery.

Can we really succeed? Can we really do it? Yes. Yes. We must.

To his left, Chase sees the Mendacium news truck parked outside a shabby barbershop. Stepping out onto the street, Samantha fixes her hair.

"Why did you get me out of bed at this hour?" Jim grumbles. His puffy eyes filled with weariness and anger. Thick morning saliva still hangs in the back of his throat.

"Because I told you Dr. Morey left for something. Didn't you see those fireworks? Something is happening. I just hope we didn't miss it."

"You're such a whore," Jim mumbles.

"Excuse me?"

"How else would you know Dr. Morey would have done anything tonight?"

"My personal life is not your concern."

"Just like Jenny was never a concern. We could have covered her stor—"

"Oh my god," Samantha grumbles, pinching the bridge of her nose, "get over Jenny. You hardly knew her."

"That's not the point. That was never the point."

"Forget it, ok?" Samantha snaps. She fixes her hair and flattens her dress. Checking her makeup in the van's side mirror, she puckers her lips.

"This isn't a beauty show," Jim grumbles.

"The better I look, the more viewers we get."

"Sure."

Standing in the middle of the road, Samantha poses like she's about to give a report. Smiling, she asks, "How do I look?"

"You loo—" Four SWAT vans tear around the street corner, interrupting Jim. Their engines growl like four bears on the hunt. Samantha scuttles towards Jim. Usurping her by the shoulders, he locks eyes with her.

"What are you doing, Jim?" Samantha asks, her eyes getting wide. Jim smiles wickedly. How he hates her. He utterly loathes her. Waiting a couple of seconds, Jim watches the first truck pass.

"Fuck despair, Sam," Jim laughs sinisterly, hurdling Samantha into the second truck. It swallows her screams with one mighty thud. A rush of bloodthirsty ecstasy fills Jim's cheeks. "I think that made me wet," he cackles. With one streamline motion, the SWAT van in the back swings around, clipping Jim. Flying face-first into the Mendacium News van, he crumbles into a broken corpse.

Picking up the pace, Oliver waves his hand in the air. They have reached the halfway point. Not quite running, the children try to keep up with Oliver, although it appears as if he's hardly exerting any effort. Already wheezing, Chase feels his throat burn. Spitting a lob of thick saliva, he clears his throat wishing that he applied himself more to athletics growing up.

"You can do this. Keep your eyes forward," Chase whispers to himself. Rounding corners onto the main road between Paddington and Boltstock, twelve SWAT vans chase the children from behind. The trucks stay in groups of four, taking up the whole width of the road.

"Oh, God, you got to help us," Chase huffs, running faster. Out of the corner of his eye, he spots a red van pulling onto the main road. Looking over at the parade of children in astonishment, Harriet shakes her head.

They escaped? It can't be. What will happen? What will happen to me? she thinks to herself until a blaring horn interrupts her thoughts. Before she can even turn around, her van crumbles like a trash compactor crushing a can. Piling up, four SWAT vans halt. Eight remain.

The children are in a full-fledged run now; their feet are practically kicking up asphalt. The gate is nearing, but so are the SWAT vans. Glancing over his shoulder, Chase notices one van sped up, breaking formation. He can't see the driver behind the tinted glass, but he swears he heard the driver call his name. Jerking the van to the right, the driver bursts open the door. A wild-eyed Peter breaks his fall with a barrel roll. Sprinting, he flaps his hand in the air urgently. Three seconds drift by until a massive collision shocks Orbis. The leading SWAT vans slam into each other, blockading the road. Wrecking into the unintentional blockade, the four vans in the back flip onto their sides. Peter, barely ahead of the crashing trucks, catches up to Chase. An ear- to-ear grin covers his face.

"Good to see you," Chase says in between deep breaths.

"Glad to make it," Peter replies. "If you excuse me, I need to say hello to Oliver." Leaving Chase behind in a cloud of dust, Peter bolts for the front of the crowd. Oliver, slowly increasing the gap between him and the children, catches sight of Peter.

"Peter!" he calls over his shoulder. Running as fast as possible, Peter's legs are just a blur. He reaches Oliver with a short burst of speed.

"Yes," he gasps. He tries to wet his dry mouth.

"Don't stop running!" he yells. Breaking free from the crowd, Oliver bolts for the gate's operation room. Out front sits a black convertible with three heavies locked and loaded. Raising their machine guns like battering rams, they aim at Oliver. Before their fingers reach the triggers, Oliver's face lights like a flash-bang grenade. Going blind, they cry out in pain as they hit their heads against the convertible. Leaping over them, Oliver yanks the operation door open. Inside, just a couple of feet from the door, is the lever to open the gate. Diving for the lever, he hears gunfire. A split second slowly passes as Oliver's fingers wrap around the lever, and the bullet travels through his skull. Laying enough weight into his dive, the lever gives, and sirens blare throughout Orbis as the gate's gears grind. The portal is opening. It's actually opening.

"No!" Dr. Morey bellows, stepping over Oliver's body. Dropping his gun, he tugs at the lever.

Snap!

Something behind the lever breaks. It jiggles like a funny-looking bobblehead.

"No! No! No!" Dr. Morey screams, slamming his fist against the concrete wall. Outside the window, he sees the children funnel through the ever-widening gate. "Impossible!" With steam spewing out his ears, he towers over Oliver's body. "At least I killed you."

A spasm cuts through Dr. Morey's face. Oliver's body starts to glow.

"What?" Dr. Morey gasps. Filling with flesh, bone, brain, and matter, Oliver's head repairs itself. "What?" The light increases in intensity. Opening, Oliver's eyes meet Dr. Morey's.

"He's alive?" Dr. Morey shakes his head. "He's alive! He's alive!" Dread sweeps across his entire body, making his legs like jelly. Blinding Dr. Morey with a flash of light comparable to the sun, Oliver rises to his feet. Fire resides in his eyes. His whole body burns like a torch with glorious rays of light.

“For the sake of freedom!” Oliver booms as the ground opens beneath Dr. Morey and it swallows his body like the barred teeth of hell.

Chapter 15

Traversing three days through the wasteland, hopes still high, Peter and Chase look at each other through their makeshift scarves. The tortuous sand beats their faces like bee stings. An uproar of wails like a troubled nursery mingle with the howling wind. The teenagers continually pass babies between themselves, hoping for just a second of quiet. The last water source they discovered was two days ago, and no food could be found. Despite being held captive for months, none of the children knew what hunger was like. Their troughs were always full.

Split into groups of ten, one sixteen or seventeen year-old a group, the children were learning how to operate as teams. Complaints were taken up with their team leader who spoke with Peter or Chase if the complaint was important enough. However, as expected, no day in the wasteland went by without trouble. Temper tantrums over hunger, pain, thirst, or all of the above were common. Plus, the tendency for small children to stray was common and resolved by having older teenagers on the edges to direct strayers back to their spots. The process took a toll on everyone, but Chase and Peter kept encouraging the children by telling them stories and reminding them of how miraculous their escape was.

Everyone quickly learned after the first week of surviving the wasteland that it isn't much different than a raging desert. The sun constantly torches the land until a giant thunderstorm passes at which point everyone tries to catch or drink as much water as possible. The days are hot, and the nights unbearably cold. One thunderstorm struck the land at night like an icy gale. Despite the necessity of water, that night proved to be troublesome.

Huddled together like weary penguins, Chase and Peter lie under the same tattered rags.

"We should have thought ahead more," Peter chatters.

"I would say so," Chase replies.

"Where do you think Oliver is?"

"I have no clue. I've just been heading straight from the gate as Oliver directed. There's hardly a way to orient ourselves beyond using the sun and stars."

"He gave me landmarks to look out for along the way, as I said. We hit some already, but there are others we have yet to reach. I swear, it feels like forever since we left Orbis."

Chase nods and says, "I agree. What do you think about the food problem? We haven't found anything to eat for a week now."

"Oliver said it wouldn't take us more than three weeks to reach our destination. We shouldn't starve, but water does prove to be an issue. We can't bank on storms. We filled enough canteens to last us a few days, but with these many kids, I don't see how they will last long."

"I don't think we have much choice. Did Oliver mention any water or food sources along the way."

"No. He just strictly charged me to follow the path he laid out and keep pressing forward."

The second week was worse. No storms drenched the land, leaving only a little water left by the end of the seven days. Groans from hunger and thirst became common from everyone; however, when a hideous creature would appear, the children fell silent out of fear. The wasteland monsters were tumorous creatures with ugly bulges across their bodies. Appendages stuck out everywhere, and their teeth were colossal. Luckily, most of the creatures were blind and relied heavily on scent. If the wind was in the children's favor, which it always was, the disgusting creatures paid no mind.

By the middle of the third week, they lost all water. The once high hopes depleted, and despair started to settle in. The weaker children began having hallucinations and fits of hysteria, while those that were stronger could hardly keep their eyes open. The idea of trying to return to Orbis passed between the group; some adamantly suggested it, and others merely proposed it.

"We're going to die out here if we don't get water! At least Orbis had that!" was the most common complaint. Peter and Chase tried to reason with the children and encourage them about how close they were to the promised land. They passed all the landmarks and could expect to find Oliver's home shortly. They just had to keep walking. The teenage leaders colluded, deciding to turn back in a day if no promised land was found. Peter and Chase prayed that Oliver would arrive soon, or else it would be all of their lives at stake.

Chapter 16

Squinting, Chase shades his eyes with a scabby hand. His eyesight has only gotten worse as the wasteland took a toll on his eyes. Everything in the distance is a blur, but he is sure he can see grass. Green grass, to be exact! Briefly, for a moment, he could hear music — a symphony.

"Peter," Chase croaks, "tell me, is there something in the distance?"

Raising his head, Peter pulls back the thin cloth covering his face, a tremble shoots through his body. "Chase, there it is. It's a beautiful oasis!" Peter shouts, his voice nearly cracking with delight.

"I'd run, but I don't think my legs can do it," Chase says, looking down at his shaking knees.

"I'll carry you, brother," Peter says, motioning for Chase to hop on his back. Excited chatter breaks across the children. They see it, too. Mary, running from her group leader who cries out her name, jumps next to Peter.

"Is that it?" she asks, her parched lips cracking the biggest smile possible.

"I think so," Peter says. Facing the army of children behind him, he bellows, "We're home!"

Shouts erupt across the children as they all break free from their groups for the gorgeous oasis ahead. Stepping out from behind foliage of green bushes, a star in the form of a human stands by the pool of water. He has hair like white wool. Flames blazing with passion crackle in his eyes. His legs, like polished bronze, glow with white light. He is like the sun, but a person. Keeping his eyes focused on the brilliant star, Peter runs as fast as he can. Children gallop by him with joyful words spewing from their lips. Diving headfirst into the oasis, the fastest children soak it in with pleasure washing over their scarred faces. A peculiar thing begins to happen. The water stirs, and the scars, bruises, and cuts across the bodies of the children in the pool heal.

Seeing this happen, the children outside the giant oasis leap into it like cannonballs. Fulfilling their thirst, they feel their strength return to their youthful bodies. The infants, when dipped into the pool, are also filled and healed. The tears cease to flow from their eyes.

"Are you ready for this?" Peter shouts.

"Of course!" Chase hollers back. Twisting, Peter jumps into the water with his back first. Chase lets go of Peter, letting the refreshing water rush over his body. Gasping, Chase expects to hold his breath, but the water is unlike the water at home. It doesn't choke your lungs. One could lay on its sandy bed and never drown. Growing stronger, Chase's stomach fills. His eyes sharpen, and the blurriness once there turns into clarity. Swimming to the surface, he laughs with the joviality of a newly wedded wife. Not a single person remains outside the oasis; thousands of bobbing heads splash each other in the delectable water. The infants, still in the arms of their elected caregivers, giggle merrily as they are sprayed with the soothing water.

"Well done, Chase," a voice booms. Swiveling in the water, Chase sees that the star-man is Oliver in his purest form.

"Oliver!" Chase shouts, swimming for the shore. Peter is right behind him. Running into Oliver's arm, Chase envelopes his body with a soaking wet hug. Peter does the same, wrapping both in his arms.

"You persevered," Oliver says approvingly. His voice is full of pride. Chase is at a loss for words. He can't believe it. He just can't believe it. It's real.

"Where's your father?" Peter asks. "Is he here?"

"Of course," Oliver laughs, "follow me." Leaving the children behind, Chase and Peter follow Oliver through a forest by the oasis. Weaving in between the lush trees, they eventually reach a glade. At the other end of this glade, a tall man prunes a couple fruit trees that are ripe. Plucking an apple, he savors the smell of the sweet fruit before biting into it.

"Father!" Oliver calls.

Turning around, Oliver's father smiles. He, like his son, shines, but his body is much larger. Standing on feet like fine gold, he wears a polished crown like that of crimson jasper with gold specs at its tips. A golden sash lies across his white raiment as well.

"Chase and Peter!" Oliver's father proclaims, opening his arms wide. "Welcome home!" Hugging all three of them, Oliver's father hums happily.

"So, you're Christian?" Chase asks as soon as Oliver's father lets go.

Chuckling, Oliver's father nods, "That I am."

"How is that possible?"

"That is a story for another time," Christian says. "I assure you it is a good one." Plucking a ripe peach from one tree and a ripe apple from the other, Christian hands the apple to Peter and the peach to Chase. With a twinkle in his eye, he says, "Eat and be filled." Peter and Chase do so, and the fruits taste like heaven. Wrapping his arms around them, Christian faces them towards the sun where Orbis also is. Oliver stands by their side as well.

"You see the sun?" Christian asks. Nodding their heads, with mouths full of sugary fruit, Chase and Peter nod. "It hangs over Orbis at this very hour. A new day has come."

"What do you mean?" Chase asks.

"This is only the beginning of my mission. Soon, when the time comes, those children will grow into mighty warriors. Orbis will one day be led out of their depravity into my kingdom. A kingdom running with milk and honey."

"That seems impossible."

"It is if Orbis has to depend on itself. Thankfully, it doesn't."

Nodding, Chase takes another bite out of his peach. A smile spreads across his cheeks as he remembers something he heard a long time ago.

"Merry freedom," he says.

"Merry freedom," Christian echoes as they all stare at the sun.

L.T. World is a graduate of Eastern Lebanon County (ELCO) High School in Pennsylvania and a current student at Lebanon Valley College (LVC). He began writing in eighth grade when his English teacher encouraged him to pursue a writing career,and he began submitting his work to magazines and publishers during his senior year in high school. L.T.'s first book, Prophesy, was published by Crave Press. When he's not writing, L.T. enjoys reading and spending time with friends.